Carioca Fletch

BOOKS BY GREGORY MCDONALD

GREGORY McDONALD

**BLACK
STONE**
PUBLISHING

Copyright © 1984 by Gregory Mcdonald
Published in 2018 by Blackstone Publishing
Cover art by Kurt Jones
Series design by Kathryn Galloway English

Printed in the United States of America

ISBN 978-1-5385-4198-2
Fiction / Mystery & Detective / Amateur Sleuth

1 3 5 7 9 10 8 6 4 2

CIP data for this book is available
from the Library of Congress

Blackstone Publishing
31 Mistletoe Rd.
Ashland, OR 97520

www.BlackstonePublishing.com

*Dedicated with affection and admiration
to Gloria and Alfredo Machado, their family
and friends*

1

Naturally the samba drums were beating, rhythms beside rhythms on top of rhythms beneath rhythms. Especially just before Carnival did this modern city of nine million people on the South Atlantic reverberate with the ever-quickening rhythms of the drums. From all sides, every minute, day and night, came the beating of the drums.

"You cannot understand the future of the world without first understanding Brazil." That was the way the trim, forty-year-old Brazilian novelist Marilia Diniz spoke. Informative. Instinctual. Indicative. The umbrella over the café table on Avenida Atlântica shaded her eyes, leaving her mouth in the afternoon sunlight. She shrugged her thin shoulders. "Unfortunately, Brazil is beyond anyone's understanding."

Marilia sat across from Fletch in a light dress with only straps over her pale shoulders. Marilia Diniz was the rare carioca who never went to the beach.

Laura Soares, more appropriately dressed in shorts, sandals, a halter, more appropriately tanned golden brown, sat to Fletch's right. Laura would always go to the beach.

Fletch was dressed in the uniform he had learned to be innocent, egalitarian: shorts and sneakers.

In front of Marilia and Laura were glasses of beer, *chope*. Fletch had the drink he liked best in all the world: guarana.

"Now that Fletch sees the Praia de Copacabana he will never go anywhere else," Laura said. "Maybe I will never even be able to get him to come back to Bahia."

"I'll go back to Bahia anytime," Fletch said. "If your father lets me."

"He'll embrace you. You know that."

"I don't know."

"The first truth about Brazil," Marilia said, "is its absolute tolerance."

"Does Brazil tolerate intolerance?"

"I suppose so." Marilia wrinkled her nose. "You see, you cannot understand."

Across the *avenida* stretched the huge, dazzling Copacabana Beach, from the Morro do Leme to his left, to the peninsula separating Copacabana from the beaches of Arpoador, Ipanema and Leblon to his right.

On the beach, among the brightly colored umbrellas and blankets, were thousands of golden brown bodies, all ages, sexes, their swimsuits so small on them only their skin, really, was visible, exercising, taking turns at the provided chin-up bars, reclining on sit-up boards, running. Within sight on the beach, Fletch counted fourteen soccer games in progress. Small children played at the water's edge, but most of the people in the water were doing disciplined swimming. Proportionately few on the beach were resting. The temperature was thirty-three degrees centigrade, about ninety degrees Fahrenheit; it was four o'clock in the afternoon, and the people's energy shimmered up from the sand more positively than reflected the strong sunlight.

At street corners to the right and left of where they sat drummed samba bands. Boys, men, from fourteen years of age to whenever, beat on drums of various sizes, various tones as if this were their last chance to do so, ever. The band to the right wore canary yellow shorts; to the left, cardinal red shorts. Immediately around each band, pedestrians stayed to give in totally to the samba awhile, dancing on the sidewalk, up and down the curb, among the cars parked pridefully anywhere. One or two drummers might stop a moment to wipe the sweat from their chests, bellies, forearms, drink a *chope* to make more sweat, but a samba band itself never stops, when it moves, when it stays in one place. A samba band's stopping is as fatal a thought as your own heart's stopping.

And the people passing on the sidewalk in front of the café, the pedestrians, going from corner to corner, band to band, businessmen dressed only in shorts and sandals, sometimes shirts, carrying briefcases, women in bikinis lugging bags of groceries, barefoot children running with a soccer ball, walked, lugged, ran, keeping the beat of the drums in their feet, their legs, their hips, their shoulders. This moving to the samba instead of just moving gives Brazilians the most beautiful legs in the world, having a true balance, an ideal proportion between muscular calves and slim thighs. The groups of gap-mouthed begging children, the cloth of their shorts worn so it almost did not exist, kept their bare feet moving to the rhythm of the drums, making the stillness, the steadiness of their huge dark eyes the more shocking, imploring. To provide a deception of class difference for the tourists, the café waiters wore black long trousers and white open shirts and real shoes, but even in their brushing crumbs from the tables, begging children away from someone they had implored too long, they somberly kept the samba beat.

"*Cidade maravilhosa!*" In his chair, Fletch stretched his arms over his head.

"Mysterious city," said Marilia. "Mysterious country."

Fletch said: "The guidebook says something like, 'At first sight of Rio de Janeiro, instantly you forgive God for what's visible of New Jersey.'"

"I like New Jersey," said Laura. "Isn't that where Pennsylvania is? I thought so."

"If you cannot understand the future of the world without first understanding Brazil," Fletch said, "I would like to understand more of Brazil's past. Granted, I came to Brazil rather quickly, without really expecting to, without being prepared, but once here I can find out very little of Brazil's history. Even Laura's father—"

Laura giggled and put her hand on his thigh. "Brazil has no past. That's what makes us so mysterious."

Marilia shot a glance at Laura. "You have not heard of *queima de arquivo?*"

A begging child came by and placed one peanut in front of each of them.

Laura laughed. "A while ago a Brazilian airliner crashed on a runway. As anyone's airliner might. Within minutes a crew showed up to paint over the Brazilian ... how-do-you-call-them? insignias on the airplane. It is our way of preventing what has already happened."

"It means 'burn the record,'" Marilia said.

"It means 'cover up,'" Laura said. "It is the Brazilian way of life. That is why we are so free."

"It has happened more than once," Marilia said. "A government takes power. In disapproval of all that has gone before, it burns the records of previous governments. Like confession, the idea has been to give us a fresh beginning."

"So we are a nation of anarchists," laughed Laura. "We are all anarchists."

"All histories are shame-filled," Marilia said.

"Brazil's shames we have expunged by setting fire to them, sending them on the wind."

At a little distance from them, the pixie, a boy about six years old, watched them with disappointment. They were not eating their peanuts.

Marilia put her sunglasses on her nose and sat back in her chair. "And you, Fletcher?"

Slowly, Fletch ate his peanut.

Instantly the small boy stepped forward and offered to sell Fletch a bag of peanuts.

Fletch took cruzeiros out of his sneaker and gave too many to the boy.

He opened the peanut bag and held it out to Marilia.

She shook her head. "Do you practice *queima de arquivo*? Are you in Brazil to burn your record?"

"Many are."

"It would make him Brazilian," Laura said. "Honorary Brazilian."

"Is that why Laura's father does not like you?"

"My father likes him," said Laura. "Loves him. It's only that—"

"Her father," Fletch said, "is a scholar. A professor at the university. A poet."

Now a dozen begging children were around his chair, whispering at him.

"Of course. Otavio Cavalcanti. I know him well. Laura is almost my niece. She should be staying with me, here in Rio."

"He is intolerant of North Americans. I am a North American."

Standing on the sidewalk near the curb, standing uncommonly still, was an old woman, a hag. A long, shapeless white dress hung from her neck. Dark pouches high in her cheekbones made it seem as if she had four dark eyes. All four eyes were staring at Fletch.

"That's not it, precisely," Laura said. "Fletcher can come here to Brazil, to sit in this café, drink guarana and watch the women walk. My father is not permitted into the United States of the North anymore, to read his poetry at Columbia University. My father is intolerant of that."

"I have read your father," said Fletch. "He speaks on behalf of the people."

Across the sidewalk the woman in white was staring at Fletch as if he had dropped from the moon.

"And there is something else." Laura shifted in her chair. "You must admit it, Fletch."

"What is it?" Marilia asked.

"My father feels Fletch does not see the difference in the Brazilian people."

"There is no equality like Brazilian equality," Fletch said. "I love that."

"It is not the equality …" Uncomfortably, Laura was looking at Marilia.

"Oh, yes," Marilia said.

"My father says Fletch keeps trying to understand the Brazilian people through other people he has known. He cannot see the other side of us."

"There is much I don't understand," Fletch said.

"There is much you do not accept."

Fletch grinned at his own joke: "There is much I cannot see."

"My father—"

"Your father is a member of a *candomblé*," Fletch said. "An intelligent man like that."

Marilia twisted the cloth braided around her left wrist.

"But he loves Fletch. He says Fletch is surprisingly open, as a person," Laura said.

"As a North American."

"You cannot understand Brazil," Marilia said from behind

her sunglasses. "Brazil accepts thieves. The United States of North America will not accept scholars and poets who speak on behalf of the people."

"Am I a thief?" Fletch asked. Clearly the hag staring at him from across the sidewalk thought he was something extraordinary.

"You said you came here rather quickly."

"True."

"You said you did not expect to come here. You were not prepared."

"True."

"You do business with Teo da Costa."

"True."

"Teodomiro da Costa is my good friend. In fact, I understand I will see you both at dinner at his house tonight."

"Good."

"Teodomiro da Costa makes a good business changing hard currencies, like dollars, into cruzeiros, into hard commodities, like emeralds, gold. He has become very rich doing so."

At the word cruzeiros, the pixies around Fletch stepped even closer and raised the pitch of their imploring whispers.

Fletch said, "I thought he drove a taxi."

"Teodomiro da Costa does not drive a taxi."

Fletch took more money from his sneaker and gave it to Laura to pay the waiter. When Laura paid, speaking Brazilian Portuguese, the bill was sometimes as much as ninety percent less. He gave some cruzeiros to the smallest begging child.

"Marilia," Laura said. "In Brazil, a man's past is burned."

"You may burn Fletcher's past," Marilia said. "That is all right. Laura, I do not want to see you burn your future."

"There is no future, either," said Laura. "There is the piano."

"The Brazilians wish for a future," Marilia said.

"Past ... future," Fletch muttered.

"I said something wrong," Laura said.

"You are staying at the Yellow Parrot?" Marilia asked.

The Hotel Yellow Parrot was on Avenida Atlântica and known to be among the most expensive.

"Yellow Parrot," said Fletch. "You must admit some things in Brazil do not make sense."

"Fletch is okay," Laura said. Then she said something rapidly in Portuguese. "My father loves him."

Down the sidewalk to the right, stepping warily around the samba band sweating in canary yellow shorts, through the dancers, came a North American woman, clearly from the United States, clearly newly arrived, in a light green silk dress moving on her body as she moved, green high-heeled shoes, wearing sunglasses, and stupidly carrying her purse like a symbol of rank dangling from her forearm: the California empress.

Laura put her hand on Fletch's forearm. "You okay, Fletch?"

"My God! I mean, why not?"

"Suddenly you turned white."

"Let go of me." Fletch flung off her hand.

He ducked beneath the table and began retying his sneakers.

Instantly there were the seven or eight heads of the pixies under the table with him, to see what he was doing.

Laura's head joined him under the table, too. "Fletch! What's the matter?"

"Estou com dor de estomagô!"

The pixies groaned in sympathy for him: "Oooooooohh!"

"You are not sick from the stomach!" Laura said.

"Estou com dor de cabeça!"

"Oooooooohh!"

"You are not sick from the head!"

"Febre … nausea … uma insolacao …"

"Oooooooohh!"

Seen relaxed in the shade under the table, Laura's legs were great to look at. Marilia's, although pale, were not so bad either. The sight made him feel better.

"Fletcher! What is the matter with you? Why are you so suddenly under the table?"

"That woman. That woman in green passing by. Don't look now."

The heads of the pixies looked back and forth from Fletch to Laura intelligently, as if they understood.

"So? What about her?"

"She probably thinks I murdered her husband."

2

"*Janio!*" With a frightening rush of long white dress through heavy green leaves, the old hag emerged from the bushes in front of them in the small forecourt of the Hotel Yellow Parrot. She was pointing her arm, her arthritically bent index finger at Fletch's face. "*Janio Barreto!*"

Fletch took a step back. His hand gripped Laura's arm.

The hag took a step forward, her finger in Fletch's face. "*Janio Barreto!*"

He thought they had done quite well. They had left Marilia at the café, walked half a block to their right, through the samba band on that corner, ignoring the gestures to stay and dance for a while, turned right, right again on Avenida Copacabana, along that a few blocks, turning right again at the street just beyond the Hotel Yellow Parrot, carefully, looking first, hurried around the corner and the short way along the sidewalk and into the forecourt of the hotel. They were to use the beach entrance to the hotel, as Fletch was not wearing a shirt.

He had forgotten about the hag.

Now she was blocking their way into the hotel entrance.

"Janio Barreto!" she accused, wagging her bent finger in his face. "Janio Barreto!"

Laura stepped forward. She put her hand on the old woman's sleeve and spoke in a soothing voice. Fletch recognized the Portuguese word for *mother* in what Laura said.

"Janio Barreto!" the hag insisted, pointing at him.

Laura spoke quietly to the woman some more.

The uniformed doorman appeared through the main door of the hotel and came through the forecourt to Fletch. "Is there a problem, sir?"

"No. I don't think so. I don't know."

The two women were talking quietly.

"Give her some money," the doorman said. "For charity."

The hag was speaking rapidly now, to Laura.

The old woman kept glancing at Fletch. She was fairly tall and fairly slim, and clearly she could move fast to have gotten to the hotel before them, to have caught them. The leanness of her hands made her fingers seem all the more misshapen. Her brown eyes were huge, clear and intense; her face more wrinkled than drying, caked earth. Thin, iron-gray hair fell from her head like photographed lightning. Her high, cracked voice came through a few blackened teeth.

Now Fletch was hearing the Portuguese words for *wife, husband, father, sons, daughter, boat.*

Listening to the old woman, Laura began taking long, surmising looks at Fletch. Her looks seemed unsure—not of what the old woman was saying, but somehow of Fletch. She was looking at him as if she had never seen him before, or seen him in quite this way.

His face politely averted, the doorman was listening too.

"What is she saying?" Fletch asked.

Laura waited until the old woman finished her sentence.

"She says you are Janio Barreto."

"Who? What?"

"Janio Barreto."

"Well, I'm not … whatever. Whoever. Let's go."

Laura's chin came forward a few centimeters. "She says you are."

The hag spoke some more, clearly repeating what she had said before, something about a boat.

Looking into Fletch's eyes, not smiling, Laura said, "She says you are her husband."

"Her husband. Ayuh."

Laura repeated with firmness: "She says you are Janio Barreto, her husband."

Now Laura had the old woman's hands cupped in her own, gently, protectively.

"Of course," said Fletch. "Naturally. Certainly. She's not the first to say that, you know. Or the second. Tell me, does she have a settlement lawyer in California?" The doorman, having heard all, having understood all, turned his head and looked at Fletch. "Tell her she'll have to get in line with her settlement lawyer."

He smiled at the doorman.

The doorman was not smiling at him.

Laura said, "You are her husband, Janio Barreto."

"Hope she sues for settlement under that name. What is this? What's going on? Laura!"

Laura said, "You died forty-seven years ago, when you were a young man, about as you are now. When you were this lady's young husband."

"Good grief."

"You are, how do I say it? Janio Barreto's aura. His other person. His same person." Laura smiled. "She is glad to see you."

"I can tell." Standing in the little forecourt of the hotel, surrounded by thick, deep green bushes, hearing the cars going by in the avenida, the voices of the children playing, hearing, of course, the beatings of the samba drums, Fletch felt coldness breaking over him, prickling his skin. "Laura ..."

Still gently holding the woman's hands, Laura said, "With this woman you have two sons and a daughter. Grown now, of course. They have children of their own. She wants you to meet them."

"Laura, she wants money. I'm not taking on an extended Brazilian family."

The doorman was still studying Fletch.

"You were a sailor," Laura said. "You earned your living from the sea."

The old woman had turned, was facing Fletch, presenting herself to him.

Quietly, Laura said, "She wants to embrace you."

"Laura! My God ..." Fletch could not help himself from moving somewhat backward, somewhat sideways. There were tears on the old woman's cheeks. Laura had let go of the old woman's hands. He felt a branch of one of the bushes against his bare back. "Laura, what is this? What are you doing?"

"The important thing is ..."

The old woman came to Fletch. She raised her arms, put them around his neck. Approaching him, her eyes were soft, loving.

"Laura!"

The doorman held up his hand as if to stop traffic. "Wait, sir. There is more."

The hag's cheek, wet with tears, was against Fletch's. She smelled terribly, of cooking oils, of fish, and of a million other things. Her body pressed against his.

He did not want to breathe. He wanted to gag. The branches from the bushes were stabbing into the skin of his back.

"The important thing is ..." Laura's head was lowered. She

spoke respectfully. "Is that forty-seven years ago, when you were a young man, in another life, you were murdered."

From the back of his throat, Fletch coughed over the old woman's shoulder.

Then Laura looked up at Fletch, her brown eyes moving rapidly from his left eye to his right to his left. "Now you must tell your family who murdered you!"

Also with his eyes on Fletch's, the doorman nodded solemnly.

Her eyes settled in Fletch's, Laura said, "Clearly you cannot rest until you do."

3

"Of course," Fletch said, coming out of the bathroom, a towel wrapped around his waist, "I really don't know how reasonable I want you to be."

"I am very reasonable."

Naked, long, lean, she lay across the rumpled white sheets of the bed reading *Newsweek*. Her wavy black hair fell over her face. The late afternoon sun through the shaded balcony window made consistent the gold in her skin.

"Laura Soares," he said. "From São Salvador da Bahia de Todos os Santos. Studied piano at the university in Bahia, then two years at the London Conservatory."

"I did not like London Conservatory. There is little understanding of Brazilian music there. In a conservatory they conserve music, you know? They don't like to let it expand."

"Sometimes gives concerts. Daughter of Otavio Cavalcanti, scholar and poet. And your mother cultivates orchids and takes photographs."

"My mother grows flowers and takes pictures of them. She is trying to beat time."

Fletch opened the shade more. Their room was at the back of the hotel, overlooking utility areas. Through tall windows in the building across the area, Fletch watched a man painting a room. The man, in undershirt and shorts, had been painting the room during the day and well into the evening since they had arrived at the Yellow Parrot. It looked an ordinary, albeit big, room. The man was either a meticulous painter or had no other work waiting for him.

Fletch said nothing for a moment.

He had gone directly into the shower. The odor of the old woman had clung to him. His face was sticky from her tears, the back of his neck pasty from her caresses.

He had gotten himself thoroughly soaped when the shower curtain drew back and Laura stepped in. She helped him wash, even putting him on his knees in the bathtub, doubling him over, to scrub the back of his neck. She was kneeling before him in the bathtub, the shower water cascading off her head, shoulders, breasts. He began to clean her thighs with his tongue.

After they messed up the bed and each other to the sound of the samba drums coming through the windows, and lying quietly awhile until the sweat dried and made him feel cool, he went back into the shower.

Standing at the window he said, "Questions …"

Reading from the magazine, the lean, naked Laura said, "Half your diet should be carbohydrates."

"You're reading about diets? You don't need to improve yourself."

"My mother will be glad to hear about the carbohydrates. Am I saying 'carbohydrates' right?"

"No. But I understand."

"I don't think they talk about carbohydrates in London. I never heard the word. Pasta!"

"Don't you have any questions?" he asked.

"About pasta?" Still she did not look up from the magazine.

"About the woman in the green silk dress. I told you she probably thinks I killed her husband. She's come here to find me."

"So?"

"You haven't asked me about that."

"That has to do with your past. Anyone can make up a story and say it is the past."

"You're not curious?"

"About the future. What time is it?"

He looked at his watch on the bureau. "Nearly seven."

"We cannot be too much on time at da Costa's for dinner. It is not polite to the servants. It gives them too much to do at once. Makes them nervous."

"I have questions."

"Probably. You are a North American."

"Your father is Otavio Cavalcanti. You are Laura Soares."

"That is the past, Fletcher old top."

"I don't get it."

"It has to do with who had the name in the past. Then you forget it. This article says you should eat much more chicken and fish than red meat. It says nothing of rice and beans. *Feijoada*."

"Are you going to talk to me about that old woman?"

"Forget it, for now. She is not Yemanjá."

"I am not Janio Barreto. Whoever."

"She says you are. She recognized you. She says she studied you carefully while we were at the café. Did you notice her?"

"Yes."

"She said you have the identical legs of her husband, the same stomach muscles from pulling the fish nets, the same proportion between your shoulders and your hips. She said the slight slash of your navel is identical."

"Laura ..."

"Well, she should know."

"I have never pulled fish nets."

"You have the muscles from Janio Barreto."

"Laura, not many Brazilians have my basic light coloring."

"Some do. Janio Barreto did. Your heads are identical, she says, your eyes."

"I had a similarity to the husband of the woman in the green dress, too."

"Similarity has nothing to do with it. She says you are Janio Barreto, her husband."

"Who was murdered forty-seven years ago."

"Yes."

"I'm a ghost? Is that what she's saying?"

"Partly that. No, you are yourself. You are Janio Barreto. You see, you came to Brazil. You see why, don't you?"

Fletch exhaled deeply. "What is the old woman's name?"

"Idalina. Idalina Barreto."

"What bothers me is that you listened to her. The doorman—"

"Why not?" Laura turned the page of the magazine. "She was talking."

"Laura, you seem to have no regard for the real past. Yet you listen to these impossibilities."

She was studying some health chart in the magazine. "What's real?"

"Which is more real to you?"

"Bananas are good for potassium," she said. "I think I knew that."

"You won't let me explain. You won't explain to me."

"Forget Idalina Barreto, as much as you can, for now."

She flung the magazine aside and looked at him standing between the window and the bureau.

"How are we to know each other?" he asked.

She rolled more onto her back and held one leg, one arm in the air. "By sharing your banana with me."

He laughed.

"I need more potassium."

"Potassium gluconate, I hope."

"Come, come, Janio. I want some more of your potassium."

"I'm not Janio."

"Janio's potassium. Your potassium. Harvest your banana and feed me your potassium."

"You're crazy."

"Come, come, my Janio. It is ripe. I see that it is ripe. I will peel it with my teeth. Let me taste your banana."

"WHERE'S MY SHOE?" He regretted kneeling on the floor in his long white trousers to look under the bed for his shoe.

She came into the room and stopped. In the bathroom she had bathed and done her hair and also dressed in white slacks and an open white shirt.

"Why is this stone under our bed?"

Sitting back on his haunches, he showed her the small carved stone he found under the bed. "It's a toad. It looks like a toad."

"That," she said.

"Why is there a stone toad under our bed?"

"The maid must have left it there."

"The maid left a stone toad under our bed?"

"Put it back," Laura said. "It may be important to her."

4

"My father's here!" Laura dumped three teaspoonfuls of sugar into her cachaça. "I hear his voice."

Courteously, Fletch took his glass of cachaça from the silver tray held out to him by a houseman. Cachaça is a brandy made of sugar-cane juice. In Brazil it is courteous to offer guests cachaça. It is courteous of guests to accept cachaça. Fletch had tried it with some added sugar, much added sugar, no added sugar. Cachaça was a taste he had not acquired.

With his glass of cachaça in hand, he followed Laura out onto the terrace.

Teodomiro da Costa's house was built somewhat upside down. Entering at street level, one went downstairs to the bedrooms and a small family sitting room, upstairs to the grand living room filled with splendid paintings and other objets d'art, upstairs again to a huge reception room complete with full bar. Off the reception room, high above Avenida Epitácio Pessoa overlooking the truly beautiful lagoon Rodrigo de Freitas, was a handsome terrace decorated with green, red, yellow flowering jungle plants.

Now in the reception room a long table had been set with crystal and silver for twelve.

Teodomiro da Costa did well exchanging currencies and commodities. Fletch had invested his money with him.

On the terrace Laura and Otavio were greeting each other with hugs and kisses and rapid talk in Brazilian Portuguese.

Wordlessly, Otavia then shook Fletch's hand.

"*Boa noite*," Fletch said.

"Otavio has come here to meet with his publisher," Laura said. "He is staying nearby, with Alfredo and Gloria. Have you met them? Alfredo is a marvelous man, true Brazilian, so full of life, generous to a fault. Gloria is a marvelous woman, truly bright, so charming, with a large feminine soul."

"Are they here?"

Laura looked around at the other people on the terrace. "I don't see them."

"They are preparing for the Canecáo Ball tomorrow night." Otavio said. "I do not need to prepare. Poets are born in disguise."

"And your mother?" Fletch asked Laura. "She did not come from Bahia?"

"My mother," said Laura. "Orchids you can never leave."

"They are worse than children," agreed Otavio.

"Worse than I was, anyway," Laura said.

Teodomiro da Costa came across the terrace to them. He was a tall man of sixty with the head of a bald eagle. "Fletcher, it is good to have you back. Did you enjoy Bahia?"

"Of course."

"Good. For dinner we are having *vatapá*, a typical dish from Bahia."

Fletch smiled and took Laura's free hand. "I made friends there."

"But Cavalcanti is my friend." Teo kissed Laura on the cheek. "And Laura too."

Otavio said, "We are all friends."

Teo took Fletch's cachaça and placed it on the tray of a passing houseman. He said something to the housewoman. "I have ordered you a screwdriver," he said to Fletch.

"Is it called a screwdriver in Portuguese?"

Teo laughed. "I called it orange juice, vodka, and ice."

"I must figure out the words for it."

"Not hard."

"To say it rapidly. With firmness."

"Come. I want you to meet da Silva." Slowly Teo guided Fletch by the elbow across the terrace. "Is Laura with you, or with her father?"

"With me."

"Ah! You are so lucky." Teo then introduced Fletch to another sixty-year-old businessman, Aloisio da Silva.

Immediately, da Silva said, "You must come to my office. I have a new computer system. The very latest. Digital. From your country."

"I would be very interested in it."

"Yes, you must come tell me what you think."

The houseman brought Fletch his screwdriver.

"Also, perhaps you have noticed my new building going up. How long have you been in Rio?"

"I was here for three weeks, then I was in Bahia for two weeks. I am back three days."

"Then perhaps you have not noticed my building?"

"Rio is so vibrant."

"Of course. It is in the Centro. Near Avenida Rio Branco."

"I did notice a new building going up there. Very big."

"Very big. You must come and see it with me. You'd be very interested."

"I'd like that."

"It is amazing what a difference computers make when it comes to building a building."

Marilia Diniz appeared with her glass of cachaça. She kissed Aloisio and Fletch on their cheeks.

"Are you well, Aloisio?"

"Of course."

"Rich?"

"Of course."

Marilia forever remained a surprise to Fletch. She had to be the only person in Rio with no sun-color in her face. She saw people from a different perspective.

"Marilia," Fletch said. "Something happened to us after we left you."

"Something always happens in Rio." She sipped her cachaça. "Listen. Teo has some new paintings. He has promised to show us them after dinner."

"Otavio, perhaps you would help me to understand something."

"Yes?"

Fletch and Otavio Cavalcanti stood alone at the edge of the terrace, looking at the moonlight on the lagoon. Otavio was drinking Scotch and water.

In Brazil, even distinguished scholars and poets are to be called by their first names.

"Does the name 'Idalina Barreto' mean anything to you?"

"No."

"She is not a famous eccentric?"

"Not that I know."

Laura was across the terrace talking with the Vianas.

"I wonder if it is a scam."

"A what?"

"A swindle. Some sort of confidence trick."

"Ah, yes. Trick."

"This afternoon Laura and I were accosted by an old woman, a *macumbeira* of some sort, maybe, dressed in a long white gown, an old woman. She said her name is Idalina Barreto."

From the terrace the samba drums could be heard only faintly.

"Yes?"

"She said I was her husband."

Otavio turned his head to look at Fletch.

"Her dead husband. Janio Barreto. A sailor. Father of her children." "Yes …"

"That Janio was murdered when he was young, at my age, forty-seven years ago."

"Yes."

"Are you hearing me?"

"Naturally."

"She demands that I tell her who murdered me."

Otavio was looking at Fletch as had Laura, as had the doorman at the Hotel Yellow Parrot. Then his eyes shifted in a circle around Fletch's head.

"Will you help me to understand this?"

Then Otavio took a drink. "What's there to understand?"

AT THE LONG TABLE at dinner they talked of the magic in much Brazilian food which provides so much energy, the masses of sugar usually placed in the coffee, in the cachaça, the sweetness of cachaça anyway, the *dende* oil in the *vatapá* they were having for dinner. The drink, guarana, is without alcohol and also gives energy. It was said by the Indians that it cleared the blood channels going to and coming from the heart. Fletch had discovered that it relieved tiredness.

Down the table, Laura said, "Bananas are good for you, too. There is potassium in bananas."

THEN MARILIA ASKED about the paintings Teo had bought.

"I'll show them to you after dinner. Perhaps, first, Laura will play for us."

"Please," said the Viana woman.

"Certainly."

"Then I will show them to you," Teo said.

Aloisio da Silva asked Fletch, "Have you visited the Museu de Arte Moderna?"

"Yes."

"I should think you'd be very interested in that building."

"I am very interested in the building. It is a wonderful building. And I had a splendid lunch there." The people at table became silent. "There were few paintings in the museum when I was there."

"Ah, yes," Marilia said.

"I was thinking of the building," Aloisio said.

"There was a fire ..." Teo said.

"All the paintings were burned up," the Viana woman said. "Very sad."

"Not all. A few were left," Viana said.

Aloisio blinked at his plate. "I was thinking the building would interest you."

Fletch said, "The paintings in the museum got burned. Is this another case of *queima de arquivo*?"

The silence at the table was complete.

From the head of the table, Teodomiro da Costa looked down at Fletch. A virus a few years before had given da Costa's left eye a permanent hooded effect, which became worse when he was tired, or wished to use it on someone. He was now using it on Fletch.

"It is a good thing, I think," Fletch said into the silence, "for the artists of each generation to destroy the past, to begin again. I think perhaps it is necessary for them."

It was many moments, then, before conversation flowed smoothly again.

"You have Laura, I see. I am glad." Viana sat next to Fletch on the divan in the living room. They were waiting for Laura Soares to play the piano. "You must be very careful of women in Rio."

"You must be very careful of women everywhere."

"That is true. But women in Rio." He sipped his coffee. "Even I. Late at night. Have found myself dancing with one of them. A man, you know. An operated-on man. It is more easy than you think to be tricked."

"Not anything is as it seems in Brazil," Fletch said.

"It is easy to be tricked."

Laura played first some Villa-Lobos, of course, then some of her own arrangements of the compositions of Milton Nascimento, somehow keeping in balance his romantic sweetness, his folkloric virility, his always progressing, complicated, mysterious melodic lines. At the side of the room, in a deep armchair, Otavio Cavalcanti dozed over his coffee cup. Then she played arrangements of other deeply folkloric Brazilian music Fletch did not recognize.

Laura Soares must have used piano technique she learned at the London Conservatory, but she played none of the music she had learned there.

After everyone except Otavio, her father, had applauded, Laura said, "Not so good." She smiled at Fletch. "I have practiced little the last two weeks."

"We have come to see your new paintings, Teo!" So the young man first into the reception room announced. With his white open shirt and slacks he wore a forest green cape, a green buccaneer hat, green shoes. Immediately, his eyes found Fletch across the room.

"I've been waiting for you," Teo said from the bar.

Just suddenly they were there, four young men dressed expensively, tailored perfectly, each in his own style, moving slowly, expectantly into the big reception room at the top of the house like a theatrical troupe taking over a stage. All but one had lithe bodies, the graceful ways of moving one would expect from fencers, acrobats, or gymnasts. The fourth was heavier, duller in the eye, maybe a little drunk, and moved unevenly.

"Toninho!" the women cried.

The Viana woman smothered him with kisses.

"Tito! Orlando!" No one seemed to greet the fourth young man immediately. Someone finally said, "Norival! How do you find yourself?"

Tito was dressed entirely in black. His shirt and slacks had to have been fitted to him while they were wet. No seams showed in his clothes.

Orlando wore blue stripes down the sides of his white slacks, blue epaulets on his shoulders.

And Norival was dressed as expensively, but somehow the earth-brown pockets in his light green slacks and shirt did not seem so amusing.

The people had surrounded the four young men, three of whom were uncommonly handsome, and were talking in Portuguese and laughing. Laura had gone to give each of them a hug and kisses.

Fletch ordered a guarana from the barman.

Not only had the dinner been cleared from the long table in the reception room during Laura's recital, the long table itself had disappeared.

Their backs to the room, some paintings had been placed on the floor along one wall.

One easel had been set up in the best light of that room.

Now Toninho stood in that light, in front of the easel, making gestures with his arms which made his green cape ripple in that light. Whatever he was saying was making the people around him laugh. He seemed to be charming even his companions, Tito, Orlando, and Norival.

Laura's eyes were shining happily when she came back to Fletch.

"Who are they?" he asked.

"The Tap Dancers. They are called the Tap Dancers. Just friends of each other. It's just a name."

"Do they dance?"

"You mean, professionally?"

"Yes."

"No."

"Sing?"

"No."

"Do tricks?"

"They are just friends."

"Fashionable, I think."

"Aren't they sleek?"

Hand emerging from his cape, Toninho came forward to shake hands with Fletch.

"Toninho," Laura said happily. "This is I. M. Fletcher."

"Ah, yes." Toninho's eyes were as brilliant as gems and as active as boiling water. "Janio Barreto. I am Toninho Braga."

"You know about that?" Fletch shook hands.

Toninho flung his arms up, sending his cape back over his shoulders. Clearly, in his eyes, he was enjoying his own act; possibly, confident in his virility, he was satirizing fashion, fashionable behavior. "The whole world knows about that!"

Teo da Costa came into the group.

Laura said something to Toninho in Portuguese. Toninho answered, briefly, and she laughed.

"Fletcher," Teo da Costa said quietly, "within the next day or so, I would like to talk with you. Privately."

"Of course."

"Your father is not here. Not looking into your life …"

With great dignity, Teo's face was averted.

"Of course, Teo. I'd appreciate it."

"Come, Teo!" Toninho exclaimed. "The paintings! We came to see your new paintings!"

ONE BY ONE, Teo placed the paintings on the easel and let his guests study, enjoy them. They were by Marcier, Bianco, Portinari, Teruz, Di Cavalcanti, Virgulino. For the most part they were clear, even bold, in the bright, solid earth colors. Especially did Fletch like one of a mother and child, another of a child with a cage. All the rhythms and colors and feelings and mysteries of Brazil were in the paintings, to Fletch.

LATER, Fletch sat on the divan next to the sleepy Otavio Cavalcanti.

"You like the paintings?" Otavio asked.

"Very much."

"Better than the museum building?" Otavio smiled. "You are a North American. Everyone expects your passion to be for buildings and computers and other machines."

"Yes."

"Teo perhaps has the best collection, now that the museum is just a wonderful building again."

"He must be careful of fire."

To that, Otavio did not respond.

"Perhaps you can tell me this," Fletch said to Otavio. "Getting dressed tonight, looking for a shoe, I discovered a small carved stone under my bed."

Otavio raised one eyebrow.

"A small stone. It was carved into a toad. A frog."

Otavio sighed.

"Why would the maid put a stone toad under my bed?"

Slowly, heavily, Otavio Cavalcanti lifted himself off the divan. He went to the bar and got himself a Scotch and water.

"COME ON." Laura samba-walked across the room, holding her hands out to Fletch. He sat alone on the divan, thinking of Ilha dos Caiçaras. He was thinking of himself as Ilha dos Caiçaras, a small island in the lagoon. "I worked enough. I played a little concert. Let's go with the Tap Dancers."

"Where are they going?"

Otavio was drinking alone at the bar.

"Seven-oh-six. Toninho wants us to go with them. To hear the music. To dance."

"Everyone?"

"Just you and me. And the Tap Dancers."

Fletch got up from the divan. "Why do I keep asking your father questions? Great scholar. I have never gotten an answer yet."

Laura glanced at her father at the bar. "Come on. If you have foolish questions, the Tap Dancers will have foolish answers for you. You'll get along fine together."

5

"Toninho must always make an entrance," Laura said in the dark nightclub. "I think he does so on purpose."

"Do you really think so?" Fletch mocked.

Fletch and Laura had driven in his yellow two-seater MP convertible directly from the sidewalk in front of da Costa's house to the sidewalk in front of 706.

The Tap Dancers had disappeared in their own black four-door Galaxie.

At the door, Laura spoke to a young waiter, and instantly three tables for two were pushed together for them. Of course the band in the club was playing. The music would be nonstop. As soon as Laura and Fletch sat at the table, a waiter brought a bottle of whiskey with a marked strip of tape down its side, a pitcher of water, a bucket of ice and many glasses.

"What did you tell the waiter?" Fletch asked through the sound of the drums.

"That the Tap Dancers are coming."

"They are that famous?"

"Everyone loves the Tap Dancers."

"They're sleek."

"Yes. They're sleek."

In a moment, they appeared in the door. Each wore the mask of a cat over his face. There were four girls with them.

Even without making noise, they soon had everyone's attention. They began to sniff up and down the walls, along the tables, through a foreign lady's bouffant, curious about everything, until they found their own table.

Even the man who was singing at the moment laughed. The sound of his laughter through the amplifier in the middle of a song was delightful.

As the catlike Tap Dancers found their table and sat down, even those who were dancing applauded them.

One squeezed in beside Fletch and took off his mask. Toninho. Fletch expressed the appreciation of having been tricked that he had learned was appropriate in Brazil.

Fletch said, "Laura suspects you make big entrances on purpose."

Smiling, face flashing even in the near-dark, Toninho took off his buccaneer's hat. "What's fun?"

Fletch said, "What's fun?"

"Moving." Toninho looked at his hand on the table, directing Fletch's attention to it. He raised and lowered his ring finger. "That's fun," he said. He raised his ring finger, little finger and thumb, and lowered them. "That's more fun." Then his hand on the table became terrifically animated, the fingers fluttering, doing their own crazy dance, the hand itself becoming some sort of a crazed rabbit trying to keep up its own wild beat. Watching it, Toninho laughed. "That's most fun."

"Have you ever had experience with paralysis?" Fletch asked. "Have you ever been paralyzed?"

Toninho's big brown eyes swelled. "I have the wisdom to know that one day I will be."

Introductions to the girls were made. Fletch got none of their names right, over the sound of the music. They clearly were glad and impressed to be there, to hear such good music, have access to the Scotch. Fletch calculated it had taken the Tap Dancers less than ten minutes to find these girls.

"Toninho," Fletch said. "Why would the hotel maid place a small carved stone toad under my bed?"

"A toad?"

"A frog."

"Was there a frog under your bed?"

"Yes. There still is."

"How do you know?"

"I found it while I was looking for my shoe."

Toninho's eyes twinkled. "What did you do with it?"

"I put it back."

"That's good." Toninho shed his cape then, and took a girl dancing to the dance floor.

For a while they all danced. The music was marvelous. Rather, Fletch danced. The Brazilians, including Laura, simply continued their being Brazilian, keeping the rhythm of the constant music anyway, their constant rhythmical movements anyway, onto the dance floor where they simply glided into full reaction to the music.

A young girl in leather jeans and a jersey which did not make it to the top of her jeans began to sing. She was extraordinarily good. They all sat at the table to listen to her.

The tape which ran down the side of the whiskey bottle was marked off in ounces. To calculate the bill, the waiter counted the ounces of whiskey missing from the bottle and charged them for that. The Tap Dancers' girls moved the whiskey level down the tape with happy alacrity.

The band did not stop when the girl put the microphone back

on its stand. Everyone stood to cheer her and she danced into the dark at the back of the nightclub.

One of the Tap Dancers' girls, who had been staring at Laura, finally asked, in Portuguese, "Are you Laura Soares, the pianist?"

"I play piano."

Tito was sitting across from Fletch.

"How did you people know about Janio Barreto?" Fletch asked him.

"About your being Janio Barreto?" Tito seemed to be correcting him.

"About that incident this afternoon."

"Is it not something to know?" Tito's face was handsome and happy too, but his eyes could not have Toninho's sparkle.

"How did you hear of it?"

Tito leaned forward across the table. "We're all very eager to hear what you will have to say."

"About what?"

"About how you came to die. Who murdered you."

"Tito, Tito. Am I never to get sensible answers?"

"Tell me one thing, Janio."

"Don't call me Janio."

"Fletch. How do you think you came to be in Brazil?"

"I am a newspaperman from California. I had an airplane ticket."

"How did you come to have the airplane ticket?"

"Sort of by accident."

"You see?"

"No. I don't see."

"Look around this room." Without moving his head, Tito shot his eyes all the way to the left and moved slowly in a straight line all the way to the right. There was something spooky in this controlled use of his eye muscles. "Do you see others here like you?"

"What do you mean?" Mostly the room was full of young Brazilians, a few older Argentinians, the foreign lady with her large bouffant and small escort.

"Other newspapermen from California who 'had an airplane ticket' and came here 'sort of by accident'?"

"Tito …"

"No. You are here."

"Why was I born?"

"Maybe that too." Tito sat back. "Now that you know what you must do, you will never rest until you do it."

"What must I do?"

"Tell us who murdered you. Murder is the most serious crime."

"Tito …"

A conspiracy of girls yanked Tito dancing.

Fletch finally poured himself a Scotch and water and sat back.

Then he and Laura danced awhile.

When it was very late in the night he found himself sitting at the end of the table with Norival, who was having difficulty keeping his eyes open and his tongue straight, being told, even being asked, about various kinds of fish available in the South Atlantic.

Slowly it occurred to Fletch that Norival was talking to him as Janio Barreto, who had fished these waters fifty years ago.

Fletch decided it was time to leave.

As he stood up, he said to Norival, "Much has changed in these waters in fifty years."

He went to the dance floor and cut in on Orlando and asked Laura if they could leave.

OUTSIDE THE NIGHTCLUB, on the sidewalk, Toninho called after him.

Fletch turned around.

Again, Toninho said, "Fletch," but he did not approach. He stayed near the door of 706.

Laura sat in the MP.

Fletch went back to Toninho.

It would be dawn soon.

"Fletch." Toninho cupped his hands around Fletch's left ear and put his lips in his cupped hands. "A woman puts a frog under their bed to keep her lover from leaving her."

Fletch stood back. "It wasn't the maid?"

"Are you the maid's lover?" Toninho laughed. He slapped his thigh with his hand. "Oh, Fletch!" He put his hand on Fletch's shoulder and shook him. "Be glad." Then he laughed again. "Also because traditionally it is a live frog!"

6

"Restless."

"Of course," she said.

This was the third time he had gotten out of bed in a half hour.

The first time, he went to the bathroom and drank from the bottle of mineral water. Then he tried snuggling up next to Laura so that all of his front touched all of her back. She breathed deeply, asleep. The second time he put his head through the drapes and saw the daylight of another morning. No electric lights were on. In bed again, he tried lying straight on his back, his hands folded across his chest as if he were in a coffin, and breathing deeply. Even at that hour, from somewhere in the city he could hear the samba drums.

Now he put on his light running shorts.

Laura raised her head from the pillows and looked at him.

"I'm going for a run on the beach," he said. "Before the sand gets too hot."

"Okay."

"I can't get to sleep."

"I know," she said. "Poor Fletch."

She put her head back down on the pillows.

7

"Can you buy me a cup of coffee?"

Joan Collins Stanwyk.

She was waiting for him, smoking a cigarette, at a little table in the forecourt of the Hotel Yellow Parrot when he came back from his run. There were three crushed cigarette butts in the ashtray on the table.

Her eyes ran over the sweat gleaming on his shoulders, chest, stomach, even on his legs.

Having finished his run with a sprint, he was breathing heavily.

"That's the least I can do for you," he said.

Two miles up the beach there had been a crew of men dressed in orange jackets fanned out like a search party cleaning the beach, and Fletch had run to them, and back. As he ran barefoot, he avoided several *macumba* fires smoldering from the night before. And he passed many dead wallets, purloined, stripped, and dropped. Even at that hour, many other people were running on the beach. And a group of Brazilian men easily in their sixties were playing a full game of soccer barefooted in the sand.

Coming back across Avenida Atlântica, the roadway was almost unbearably hot on his bare feet, and it was not yet seven o'clock in the morning.

The bar, which was the middle door at the front of the Hotel Yellow Parrot, of course was closed. Fletch pressed the service bell beside the door.

"Let's see if that brings someone." He sat across from Joan at the little table.

He folded his slippery arms across his slippery chest.

The forecourt, with thick green bushes head high on three sides, had brilliant streaks of morning sunlight in it.

This morning Joan Collins Stanwyk looked less the California empress. She was dressed in a light, tan slacks suit, white silk shirt, and sandals. Her hair was not in its usual impeccable order. Her face looked haggard; her eyes sleepless. She might still have been suffering jet lag; she might also have been suffering from her martinis and her cigarettes and, of course, from her recent widowhood.

"How are you?" he asked.

"I've been better."

"Did you come here to find me? I mean, to Rio?"

"Of course."

"How did you work it out? Where I went?"

"Did you forget Collins Aviation has its own security personnel? Mostly retired detectives who are very good at finding out things? Although, I admit, sometimes not fast enough." There was no humor in the irony of her statement. "And did you forget that I was born, bred, and educated to do a job? And that I'm rather good at it?"

She was the daughter of John Collins, who had built a mammoth airplane company out of his own garage in California. Wife, now widow, of Alan Stanwyk, the late chief executive officer of that company. A famous socialite, executive hostess for both her father and her husband, famous blond, long-legged, tennis-playing Californian beauty who had known her function in that world of fast cars and slow parties and had once, shortly before, surprised Fletch at how well she had performed, or tried to perform.

"I haven't forgotten."

A waiter appeared.

Fletch ordered coffee for Joan and guarana for himself.

She said, "You're absolutely gorgeous, wet with sweat. You have the same build as Alan had, but there is so much more light in your skin."

He tried to shave the sweat off his chest and stomach with the side of his index finger. "I don't have a towel. I've been running. I—"

A slight jerk of her head stopped him. There was something smoky about her eyes. He was looking at a woman whose life, whose whole world, had been deeply violated by circumstances, probably for the first time in her life.

"If you came here for a full explanation—"

She stopped him. "I need your help." Her hand shook before she put her fingers against her cheek and stroked the area in front of her ear. "Let's forget for now why I came here. Ironically enough, You're the only person I know in Rio, and I have to ask you to help me." Her voice was very soft.

She collected herself while the waiter set coffee in front of her, the can of guarana and a glass in front of Fletch.

"I knew you were here," Fletch said. "I saw you yesterday on the avenida. You were wearing a green silk dress. And carrying a handbag."

"Oh, yes," she said bitterly.

"I hid from you." He poured his guarana. "I was just so surprised to see you. How did you find out where I was staying?"

"I just called all the best hotels, and asked for Mister Irwin Maurice Fletcher. I knew, of course, you could afford the very best accommodations." Again, naturally, there was no humor in her irony. "Just went down the list of first-class hotels. When I asked for you here, at the Yellow Parrot, they rang your room. No answer. So I knew where you were staying."

"Why are you sitting in the forecourt waiting for me at six-thirty in the morning?"

"I had no choice. It was the next thing to do, the only thing do to. After the most horrible night ... I walked down from the hotel. While I was still up the block I saw you starting out for your run, going across the street. I wasn't about to run after you up the beach."

"No."

"I was robbed," she said.

"Oh."

"You say that with such aplomb. As if you knew it."

"I guessed it."

"How?"

"You don't know about Rio?"

"I guess not enough."

"It's a marvelous place."

"Terrific," she said.

"You going to give me all the details?"

"You sound like you've already heard them."

"I think I have."

"Robbed twice."

"Not a record."

"Robbed of everything." A tear appeared in the corner of her eye.

"Baptized," he said.

"Last night, after I found out which hotel you were in, I considered coming and camping out in the lobby until you showed up, but from what I've heard of Rio nightlife, that didn't make much sense."

"No."

"At least not for such a healthy, wealthy, attractive young man."

At first Fletch thought he would let this irony pass over him. Then he said, "I wasn't in."

"So I went out myself. I went for a walk. Right along here." She indicated the avenida beyond the hedge. "Sat in a café, had a drink, watched the people, listened to the drums. Walked further, to another café, had a drink. Couldn't pay the bill. My purse was gone."

"Yes." In his saying just "yes," Fletch heard an echo of Otavio Cavalcanti. *Yes. Of course. What is there to understand?*

"My wallet was gone. All my cash. My credit cards." Tears now were in both her eyes. "My passport."

"It happens to everyone I have heard of," he said.

"My necklace was gone!" She seemed astounded. "A diamond pin I was wearing on my dress!"

"Yes."

"What bothers me most is that pictures of Alan in my wallet are gone. Of Alan and Julia." Julia was her young daughter. "No matter what you may think, I wanted those pictures of Alan. They're irreplaceable."

Tears rolled down her cheeks.

Fletch said: "Yes."

She reached for a purse that wasn't there. "Damn! I don't even have a handkerchief."

Fletch shrugged his bare shoulders. "I don't even have a sleeve."

She sniffed.

"I explained to the waiter as best I could that I couldn't pay him. I'd been robbed. That I would come back and pay him today." Joan Collins Stanwyk sniffed again. "I swear, Fletch, all during my walk, nobody even touched me. No one bumped into me. How did they get my necklace? The pin off my dress? There wasn't even a tear in my dress. I felt nothing!"

"The future of Brazil," said Fletch, "is in surgery."

"I went back to my hotel."

"And your room had been burglarized."

"How did you know?"

"You said you'd been robbed twice."

"Everything!" she said. "Everything except my clothes. My jewel case, my traveler's checks."

"Everything."

"Everything. I haven't a thing. This morning I don't have a dollar, a cruzeiro, a credit card, a piece of jewelry."

Fletch said: "Yes."

"I went downstairs to the hotel manager immediately. The assistant manager, that time of night. He came to the room with me, clucked and hissed and *t'ched* like a barnyard, figured the thieves must have come in over the balcony, scolded me for leaving the balcony door unlocked—Good heavens, I'm on the ninth floor. It was a warm night."

"Took no responsibility."

"I spent hours with him in his office. He said I should have left all my valuables in the hotel safe. Apparently they handed me a slip of paper when I checked in with that written on it. He took me back to my room and showed me the sign on the inside of the door advising me to lock the balcony doors, to put my valuables in the hotel safe. We went back to his office. I filled out lists of things that are missing. I kept asking him to call the police. For some reason, he never called the police."

"No reason for disturbing them."

"What do you mean?"

"They've heard the story, too."

"Fletch, I was robbed. Of thousands and thousands of dollars' worth of things. Money, jewelry, my credit cards."

Again Joan Collins Stanwyk sniffed.

"The police would know all that."

"Will you help me?"

"Of course."

She clutched her hands in her lap. "I feel so violated."

"Disoriented?"

"Yes."

"Stripped naked?"

"Yes!"

"Totally lost without all your possessions?"

"Yes, yes!"

Fletch sat back in his chair. His sweat had dried in the air. "I think that's part of the idea."

"What are you talking about?"

"Who are you?"

"I am Joan Collins Stanwyk."

"Can you prove it?"

Her eyes searched the stone floor of the forecourt. "As a matter of fact, I can't. No credit cards. No checkbooks. No passport."

"How does it feel?"

"How does what feel?"

"To be whatever you are right now."

Her eyes narrowed. "I did not come to you for psychological therapy, Mister I. M. Fletcher."

"Thought I'd throw it in. No extra charge."

"I need money."

"Why?"

"I want to get out of that damned hotel. I want to pay my bill and get out of that damned hotel. I don't even have taxi fare."

"Okay. But why don't you call home? To California? Your father?"

"He's on his yacht. The *Colette*. Trying to recuperate from Alan's—"

"And you came here, to look for me."

She shrugged. "Recuperation."

"Doing your job. As you see it."

"Yes."

"Striving. Being Joan Collins Stanwyk, come hell or high water."

"Are you going to help me? I want to go—"

"Tell me. Your family has offices stuffed with people looking out for you. Security personnel. Lawyers. Accountants. Why haven't you called them?"

Her head lowered. After a moment, she said, softly, "It's Saturday. In California, it's before dawn Saturday morning."

He laughed. "And you can't wait? You'd rather come to me, whom you pursued to Rio de Janeiro, than wait until your daddy's offices open?"

"I want to get out of that hotel. That man made me so angry."

"It is essential to you, under the circumstances, that you talk to someone who knows who you are."

She blinked at him. "What?"

He put his forearms on the table. "I was robbed. Wallet, cash, driver's license. Not my passport. My watch. My Timex watch."

"Within the first twenty-four hours you were here?"

"Within the first six hours. People warn you, but you cannot believe it. You have to go through it yourself. It's a baptism."

"What do you mean, *baptism?*"

"You learn to use the hotel safe, carry what money you need immediately in your shoe. And to not wear jewelry. Not even a watch."

"Fletcher, I lost thousands of dollars, everything I have with me."

"You lost your identity."

"Yes. I did."

"You lost your past."

"Yes." Joan Collins Stanwyk was frowning at the bushes.

"Do you feel more free?"

Now she was frowning at him. "What?"

"Now you are equal, you see."

"The people who stole my possessions aren't equal."

"Oh, sure. That's widely dispersed. Come here a moment, will you?"

He got up from the table and stood in the opening of the hedge.

After a moment, she got up and came to him.

Together they looked across the city sidewalk where people were beginning to go about their daily business, across the wide city avenue filling up with taxis and commuters, to the beach, beginning to fill up with people of all ages walking, running, jumping, doing pull-ups, swimming.

Drums could be heard from down the road.

"There's not a pair of long trousers in sight, is there?" he asked.

"Very few shirts," she said.

"No wallets. No identities. No class paraphernalia: no jewelry." He looked at her tan slacks suit, silk blouse, high-heeled open-toed sandals. "They have their bodies. Their eyes, their arms, their legs, their backs."

"Their fingers, damn them."

"I think we're being told something."

"Have you gone Brazilian? In just a month?"

"Naw. I won't be carioca until I can walk across the avenida in bare feet at high noon."

She turned to go back to the table. "Sounds to me like you're giving some fantastic intellectual, political rationale for their out-and-out thievery." She sat down at the table. "But I guess you have every reason to."

"To what?"

"To understand."

"This lady I know …" Fletch too sat down at the table. "She writes novels. I doubt I've got it straight, but she told me there is some ancient ritual here, a religious ritual, for which the food, in order to be acceptable by the ritual-masters, must be stolen."

Joan Collins Stanwyk sighed. "Enough of this. I've been robbed. I need help. If I weren't desperate, I wouldn't have come to you."

"I guess so."

"Will you please come to the police station with me?"

"If that's what you want."

"I must report this."

"It won't do any good."

"Fletcher, I've been robbed, of thousands of dollars—"

"You have to pay a fee."

"What?"

"To report a robbery to the police, you have to pay a fee."

"You have to pay the police money to tell them you were robbed?"

"It's a lot of paperwork for them."

She swallowed. "Is that all it is? Paperwork?"

"Yes. I think so. In most cases." He scraped his chair legs on the stone pavement. "You are warned, you see. Robbery here is not uncommon. No one can deny that. It is also common in New York, Mexico City, and Paris."

She was beginning to have to squint into the sunlight to see him. A beam of sunlight was coming through a break in the hedge. "But here, you say, they're doing you a favor to rob you."

"You might as well think that."

"They rob you with philosophy."

"It's not considered such a bad thing to relieve you of your possessions, your identity, your past. What is yours is theirs is mine is ours ..."

Her white face was stonelike. Her jaw was tight.

He said, "I'm just trying to make you feel better."

"Fletcher, are you going to let me have some money? Right away?" Her fingers gripped her temples. Her whole head shivered. "At the moment, we won't go into the source of that money."

"Of course. I'll bring some to your hotel. I have to get out of these wet shorts and shower and get them to open the hotel safe."

"Very well."

When she stood, she looked very pale and she seemed to sway on her feet. She closed her eyes a moment.

"You all right?"

"I'll be all right."

"What hotel are you in?"

"The Jangada."

"Very posh."

"Bring lots of money."

"We'll have breakfast together. At your hotel."

"Yes," she said. "Come straight to my room with the money. Room nine-twelve."

"Right." He had been in a bedroom of hers before.

He walked with her to the break in the hedge.

"I'd send you back in a taxi," he chuckled, "but I'm not wearing shoes."

Distantly, she said, "I'd rather walk."

8

There was no answer when he tapped at the door of Room 912.

He knocked louder.

Still the door did not open.

He knocked again and then placed his ear against the door. He could hear nothing.

As quietly as possible, in his own room at the Hotel Yellow Parrot, Fletch had showered and changed into fresh shorts, a shirt, sweat socks and sneakers. Laura was still sleeping. He left a note for her, *I have gone to the Hotel Jangada to have breakfast with someone I know.*

He had driven the short distance between the hotels in his MP.

After knocking on Joan Collins Stanwyk's door at the Hotel Jangada, he went back down to the lobby and called the room on the house phone.

No answer.

At the hotel desk, he asked the clerk, "Please, what is the number of Joan Collins Stanwyk's room? Mrs. Alan Stanwyk?"

The clerk consulted his plastic-tabbed file. "Nine-twelve."

"She hasn't checked out, has she?"

The clerk squinted at his file. "No, sir."

"*Obrigado.* Where is your breakfast room, please?"

Joan Collins Stanwyk was not in the breakfast room. She was not in the bar, which was open.

On the terrace of the Hotel Jangada were two swimming pools, one which was in the morning sun, the other which would be in the sun in the afternoon. Already a few were sunning themselves around one pool. Around the pool in the shade a few were having breakfast. Two fat white men had their heads together over bloody marys.

Joan Collins Stanwyk was not in the pools area.

On the ninth floor, Fletch knocked at her door again.

From the lobby he called her room again.

At the desk, he left her a note:

Came to have breakfast with you as arranged. Can't find you anywhere. You fell asleep? Please call me at Yellow Parrot. If I'm not there, leave message. Enclosed is taxi money.
—Fletch

"Will you please leave this for Mrs. Stanwyk? Room nine-twelve."

"Certainly, sir."

Fletch watched the desk clerk put the sealed envelope in the slot for Room 912.

"Teo? *Bom dia.*" Fletch phoned from the Jangada.

"*Bom dia*, Fletch. How are you?"

"Very pleased by your new paintings. Thinking of them has made me happy."

"Me, too."

"When do you want to see me?" Three North American oil-rig

workers in heavy blue jeans got off the elevator, staggered across the lobby of the Hotel Jangada, and went straight into the bar.

"Any time. Now is fine."

"Shall I come now?"

"We'll have coffee."

9

"You do want coffee, don't you?"

"I guess I need it."

A houseman had led Fletch downstairs in Teo da Costa's house to the small family sitting room. Dressed in pajamas, a light robe, and slippers, Teo sat behind his glasses in a comfortable chair reading *O Globo*.

"Have a busy night?" Teo folded the newspaper.

"We went to Seven-oh-six. With the Tap Dancers."

"It's a wonder you've had any sleep."

"I've had no sleep."

Standing, Teo nodded to the houseman, who withdrew.

"You look fresh enough. You look like you've been out jogging."

"I have been."

A look of concern flickered across Teo's haughty face.

Fletch said, "I don't feel like sleeping."

"Sit down," Teo said. "Is there anything bothering you?"

Sitting, Fletch said, "Well, I arranged to have breakfast with this person I know, from California. When I went to the hotel, she wasn't there."

"She went out on the beach, perhaps."

"I had arranged to meet her less than an hour before I went to the hotel. She could have fallen asleep."

"Yes, of course. In Rio, night and day get mixed up. Especially as Carnival approaches."

The houseman brought two cups of coffee.

Teo sipped his standing up. "People don't realize it, but Brazil's second-largest export is tea."

After the houseman left, Fletch asked, "You wanted to talk to me, Teo. Privately, you said."

"About what you're doing."

"What am I doing?"

"What are you going to do?"

"I don't understand you."

"Brazil is not your home."

"I feel very comfortable here."

"What would you most like to do in this world?"

"Sit on Avenida Atlântica in Copacabana, eat churrasco, drink guarana, and watch Brazilian women of all ages walk. Listen to Laura play the piano. Go to Bahia, occasionally. Run, swim. Jump up and down to the drums. Love the people. I am learning a little Portuguese, a few words."

"Do you mean to stay in Brazil?"

"I haven't thought."

"How long have you been here now? Six weeks?"

"Something like that."

"You've bought a car. You've met Laura." Teo sipped his coffee. "Don't you have any plans?"

"Not really."

Teo put his cup and saucer on a table. "A young man should have plans. You're a young man. From everything I can see, a very healthy young man. You are attractive. You have a brain. Because of the business we have done together, I know how much money you have. I do not know the source of that money, but I know you are not a criminal."

"Thanks."

"I am only speaking to you, Fletch, because I am sixty, and you are only in your twenties. Your father is not here …"

"I appreciate it."

"It is not good for a young man to live without a plan."

"Are you saying I should leave Brazil, Teo?"

"Brazil is a difficult place, even for Brazilians." Teo scratched the back of his head and laughed. "Especially for Brazilians."

"Is this about Laura, Teo?" Fletch fixed Teo in the eye. "Did Otavio Cavalcanti ask you to speak to me?"

Teo used his hooded eye on Fletch. "Brazil is not that way. Not intolerant."

"Otavio is."

Teo laughed. "Otavio Cavalcanti is one of the most liberal men we have. So liberal he cannot go to New York and read his poetry at a university."

"About some things he is liberal. About his daughter …?"

"And what do you think of Otavio?"

"He is a great scholar and poet who does not answer my questions."

"Brazil is difficult to understand."

"Did Otavio speak to you last night, Teo?"

"Yes," Teo admitted. "He did. That is not what concerns me."

"Laura put a frog under our bed."

"Yes," Teo said. "So Otavio told me. You know what that means?"

"I do now."

"You see, you do not know Brazil. Perhaps cannot know Brazil. There is so much here that came from the Nago and the

Bantu, particularly the Yoruba. You can have no feeling for it."

"*Saravá Umbanda!*"

"What did you do before you came here? You were a journalist?"

"I worked for a newspaper."

"Then you must make a plan to work for a newspaper again. Buy your own small newspaper, somewhere you want to be. Understand the new technology of communications. Grow along the course you were on."

Fletch sat silently a moment.

Then he finished his coffee.

"Teo, have you heard about this Janio Barreto ... situation? That I am someone who was murdered here forty-seven years ago—?"

"Yes. I was told about it last night. It worries me."

"Why?"

"It worries me that you might not understand."

"Of course I don't understand. Perhaps you could help me to understand."

"I'm sure the woman—What's her name?"

"Idalina. Idalina Barreto."

"I'm sure the woman is entirely sincere in what she believes. There is no scam, swindle. There is no trick involved, as you asked last night."

Upstairs, a vacuum cleaner was being run.

"Teo, do you personally give any credence to such a thing?"

"Do I think you are a perispirit?" Teo smiled. "No."

Fletch said, "Phew!"

"I worry that you won't know what to do about it."

"What do I do about it?"

Teo hesitated a long moment. "I don't know either. Brazil is one of the most modern nations on earth ..." His voice dwindled off.

"I think I understand what you are saying, Teo." Fletch stood up. "I promise I will think."

"It's just that your father is not here."

"I will think of a plan."

In shaking, Teo held Fletch's hand a long moment. "The Tap Dancers," he said, "Your father would not want you to become a tap dancer on life."

"Laura?"

The window drapes were open. The room had been made up. Fletch pushed the ajar door to the bathroom all the way open.

"Laura?"

There was a note for him on the bureau.

Fletch—

Otavio called. He is feeling too tired to stay for Carnival in Rio. He wants to be home in Bahia. He said this morning he feels too tired to travel alone, through all the Carnival crowds. So I am helping him travel to Bahia.

Surely I will be back Sunday. Enjoy the Canecão Ball tonight even without me. If you get too lonely without me, I have left you Jorge Amado's *Dona Flor and Her Two Husbands*—a great Brazilian classic. And I will bring you a present from Bahia—something I want for you.

Ciao,
Laura

Across the utility area, the man was still painting the room.

The phone rang.

"Janio?"

"Not here, at present."

"Is Fletcher there?"

"Yes, he's here. I think."

"Toninho Braga, Fletch."

"How are you? Have you slept?"

"We thought you might like to spend the day with us. Drive up to a place we know in the mountains. Laura can go shopping."

"Laura's gone to Bahia with her father."

"That's well. Then will you come? A place we know, very amusing, very relaxing. It is important to get away during Carnival."

"Toninho, I haven't slept. I went running."

"This place is very relaxing. You can have a sleep there, after lunch."

"Teo da Costa is expecting me for the Canecão Ball tonight."

"Oh, we'll be back in plenty of time for that. We are going to the ball, too."

"Who's we?"

"Just Tito, Norival, Orlando, and myself. Get away from the women a few hours."

"I think I should try to sleep."

"You don't understand."

"I don't understand anything."

"We are downstairs in the lobby, expecting you."

"Toninho."

"You will come?"

Fletch looked at the freshly made bed. "*É preciso terno?*"

Such was a tourist joke. In Brazil a suit was never necessary.

"You will need no clothes. Do you have money?"

Fletch felt the wad of cruzeiros in his pocket he had taken out of the hotel safe for Joan Collins Stanwyk. "Yes."

"Good. Bring your money. We will gamble. We will gamble and take your money away from you."

"Okay."

"You coming right down?"

"Yes."

"You didn't say that."

"I'll be right down."

Before leaving the telephone, Fletch called the Hotel Jangada and asked for Room 912.

There was no answer.

He took a full liter of mineral water from the bathroom.

Before leaving the hotel room, Fletch checked under the bed.

The frog was still there.

"*Bum, bum*," Toninho said.

The black four-door Galaxie was on the sidewalk close to the hedge in front of the Hotel Yellow Parrot. Around it, dressed only in shorts and sunglasses, were the Tap Dancers. Norival, the only one with his belly hanging over his belt, held a can of beer in his hand.

"*Bom dia*, Fletch," Tito said.

"*Tem dinheiro?*"

Tito grinned. "*É para uso pessoal.*"

In front of the hotel, half in the road, half on the sidewalk, a samba band was beating its drums at full strength in the strong Saturday morning sunlight. At their center was an old pickup truck casually decorated with palm fronds, some of which had been dyed purple and red. Seated in the back of the pickup truck, facing backward, was a huge black papier-mâché monster. Its arms were out, to embrace; its eyes were big and shiny; its smile was friendly. A girl dressed only in a G-string and pasties sat on the monster's head, her legs dropping over its face. Of course she had gorgeous legs and a flat belly and full breasts. Her long black hair fell over her face. On the ground near the truck, a tall man in a long black evening gown and cherry-red face rouge danced wildly to the drums. A nine-year-old girl also danced in a black evening gown, while puffing a cigarette. A bare-legged middle-aged man danced while holding his briefcase. Perhaps there were fifty or sixty people dancing around the band.

"*Bum, bum, paticum bum,*" Toninho said.

Fletch tossed his plastic liter bottle of water onto the backseat of the Galaxie.

"Senhor Barreto," the doorman said quietly.

In one swift motion, Tito pulled Fletch's tennis shirt over his head and off him.

Orlando put his forefinger against Fletch's chest. "Look! Skin!"

"He has skin?" Norival asked, looking.

Tito ground a couple of knuckles into Fletch's back. "Muscle!"

"He is there?" Norival asked. "Really there?"

"Senhor Barreto," the doorman said, "Mister Fletcher."

"*Bum, bum,*" Toninho said.

Behind the doorman, tall, stately in her white gown, big-eyed Idalina Barreto came through the crowd. On each side of her she had a child by the hand. Three older children were in her wake. The children were clean enough, but the jerseys on the girls were too big or too small. Below his shorts, from above his knee, the ten-year-old boy had a wooden leg.

"Janio Barreto!" the hag shrieked over the sound of the samba band.

"Ah," Toninho said solemnly. "Your wife."

The doorman stood back.

Tito handed Fletch his shirt rolled up into a ball. Fletch threw it into the car.

The old woman cackled rapidly. She was presenting the children to him.

"She says they are your great-grandchildren, Janio," Tito said. "Are you catching their names? The boy is called Janio."

Fletch put his hand on the head of one of the small girls.

At first, Idalina Barreto smiled.

As Fletch ducked into the backseat of the black Galaxie, her voice became shrill. She pressed forward.

Toninho got into the driver's seat. "Aren't you going to ask your wife if you may go gambling?"

Orlando got into the front passenger seat. Entering from the other side, Tito sat in the middle, beside Fletch. Norival sat near the left window of the backseat.

Fletch handed two of the children money through his back window.

Toninho started the car. "*Bum bum*," he said.

As the car rolled forward, the hag's face continued to fill Fletch's window. Her shrieking voice filled the car.

"Ah, wives," Tito said.

Soon the car bumped off the sidewalk and got into traffic on the avenida.

Through the rearview mirror, Toninho was staring at Fletch.

There were many cans of beer on the floor of the backseat of the car.

"*Bum, bum, paticula bum*," Toninho said, driving through traffic.

"*Carnival.*" In the front seat, Orlando stretched. "How nice."

Toninho shook his head sadly. "Think of driving off and leaving your wife and great-grandchildren that way! To go gambling! What is the younger generation coming to!"

"*Um chopinho?*" Norival held out a can of beer to Fletch.

"Not yet."

Stuck in traffic, Norival handed the beer through the window to a child no more than twelve. Then he opened one for himself.

In the traffic near them was a big, modern bus. All that could be seen through the windows of the bus were bare, brown upper torsos, moving like fish in a net, the arms flailing the insides of the bus, the feet apparently stomping the floor with the rhythm, the faces raised in some song. The bus was being used as a drum, being played from the inside by more than one hundred fists, more than one hundred feet. The bus being used as a drum from the inside did not seem to impair its modern beauty or impede its rollicking progress through the traffic.

Finally the Galaxie turned into a side street and picked up speed for a short way until they came to another samba band almost clogging the street. A small seventy-year-old lady, all by herself, dressed in a red dress and red shoes, a red plastic handbag hanging from one forearm, danced to that band, taking perfect small steps with perfect dignity.

Creeping the car past the samba band, Toninho shouted through the window at them, "*Bum, bum, paticum bum, prugurundum!*"

Some of the people who heard him waved.

"*Bum, bum, paticum, prugurundum,*" Fletch tried to say. "What's that?"

"An old Carnival song," Tito said, picking a beer off the floor.

Norival was swallowing his third beer since getting into the car.

"What does it mean?"

"Nothing."

AFTER A WHILE they were free of the city, and the car began climbing the narrow, twisting mountain roads. Behind walls and hedges were suburban homes. The higher they climbed, the more expensive were the houses.

Shortly Norival had to be let out to water some of the bushes. Then he started another beer.

Occasionally through the heavy green growth, the hedges, Fletch caught glimpses of Christ the Redeemer, thirty meters tall, over a thousand tons heavy, a half mile in the sky above Rio on Corcovado, arms stretched wide to welcome and embrace the whole world. Enough times, Fletch had heard the story of the Argentine fisherman who spent days outside Baia de Guanabara waiting for the statue to wave him in. Finally, he sailed his catch of fish home to Argentina.

At one point, Toninho said in English, "You are not here long before you discover Brazilian music is not only the bossa nova of Vinicius de Moraes and Tom Jobim."

"That is for export." Norival licked the lid of his beer can.

"Perhaps Brazilian music is too complicated for others to understand," Tito said.

"The melody, too, comes from the drums," Fletch said. "People are not used to listening to the drums for melody."

For the most part, the Tap Dancers discussed which samba school would win the Carnival Parade. This matter is discussed in Brazil as fervently, as passionately, as who will win the World Football Cup or the presidential election is discussed in other parts of the world.

Each of the big favelas, slums in Rio de Janeiro, presents a finished samba school for the Carnival Parade, complete with a newly written song and huge, ornate, intricate floats; hundreds of trained, practiced drummers; brilliant, matching costumes for thousands of people. The Carnival Parade is the total competition of sound, melody, lyrics, rhythm; sights, the stately floats, dazzling costumes, the physical beauty of the people dancing from that favela, the magical quickness of the kick-dancers; originality and vitality; minds and hearts of the people of each of the slums.

All the people in each favela work all the year on their favela's presentation, being careful that their song for that year is well written, then spending many nights and every weekend practicing it, playing it, singing it, dancing it, promoting it in the streets; designing and making each of the costumes, for men and women, each more complicated than a wedding garment, by hand; designing and building their samba school float, usually as big as a mansion. Every spare moment and every spare cruzeiro goes into making each favela's presentation as beautiful, as stunning to the ear and the eye, the mind and the heart, as exciting as possible.

And the competition is most strictly judged, and therefore, of course, always the subject of much controversy.

As Fletch heard the Tap Dancers discuss these matters, which school had the best song for this year, possibly the best costumes and floats, as they knew of them, the best drummers and dancers, which did win and might have won last year, the year before, he heard the names and snatches of the songs that were now being heard everywhere, on the streets, from the radio and television. Months before Carnival, the new song of each samba school is offered the people like a campaign pledge and promoted like a political platform or an advertising slogan. The Tap Dancers discussed the various samba schools one by one, from the oldest, Mangueira, to one of the newest, Imperio da Tijuca; from one of the more traditional, Salgueiro, to the overpowering drum section of Mocidade Independente de Padre Miguel. Toninho seemed to think this year's winner would be Portela, judging the song that school was offering and what he knew of the costumes. Orlando thought Imperatriz Leopoldinense had the better song. Tito agreed with Toninho about Portela. Norival drank his beer, belched, and just said, "Beija-Flor."

Fletch wiped the sweat off his skin with his rolled-up shirt.

Breaking into English, Toninho said, looking through the rearview mirror, "Fletch, you should hope for Santos Lima to win."

"Then I do." Leaning forward, Norival gave Fletch a lopsided look. "But why should I?"

"You used to live there. That was your place. That is where Janio Barreto lived. And was murdered."

For a moment, there was silence in the car.

Then Orlando began humming the song offered this year by Imperio da Tijuca.

"ORLANDO! TONINHO!"

In the mountains, they had driven down a deeply shaded drive and pulled into the sunlight-filled parking area in front of an old run-down plantation house.

Immediately there appeared on the front porch of the house an enormous woman, a good three hundred pounds, her arms out in either greeting or sufferance, in the identical posture of Christ the Redeemer.

"Good Lord," Fletch said when he saw her through the car window.

Orlando and Toninho had gotten out of the front seat and opened the back doors.

The other side of the car, clearly Norival did not care whether he moved.

Fletch got out his side of the car. The mountain air was cooler on his skin; but, still, the sun was biting.

Around the corner of the house appeared a skinny young teenage girl dressed only in shorts. Her eyes seemed as sunken as in a skeleton's skull.

"Tito?" the woman shouted.

Tito got out of the car, grinning.

The other side of the car, Norival lumbered out, went quickly to the bushes not far away, and relieved himself.

Then behind the enormous woman imitating a statue there appeared a real statue, a mulatta, a girl six foot four easily, perfectly proportioned, an amazing example of humanity. Her shoulders were broad, her waist narrow, her legs long. Each of her breasts was as large and as full as an interior Brazilian mountain seen from the air. Each of her eyes was bigger than a fist and darker than a moonless night. Her black hair was long and flowing. Her skin was the color and texture of flowing copper. Dressed only in slit shorts and high-heeled shoes, she moved like a goddess in no great hurry to go out and sow the seeds of humanity upon a field. This amazing creature, this animate statue, smiled at them.

Fletch gulped.

"You brought me someone new!" the fat older woman yelled in English. "Is he North American? He is so beautiful!"

"He has special problems, Dona Jurema," Toninho laughed. "He has special needs!"

"My God," Fletch said. "Where am I?"

Tito punched Fletch's bicep. "At a different height in heaven."

12

"Tricked," Fletch said. "A little place we know in the mountains. You guys have brought me to a brothel."

Towels wrapped around their waists, he and Toninho were sitting in long chairs in the shade near the swimming pool. The back of the plantation house was even more dilapidated than the front. Paint was thin and chipped. The back door was lopsided on its hinges. The flower borders had gone years untended. Lilies grew in the swimming pool.

"Very relaxing," Toninho said. "I did say it was very relaxing."

"So why do the well-loved Tap Dancers need a brothel?"

"Everyone needs a few uncomplicated relationships, no? To relax."

They had entered the plantation house, each being fondled by the massive Dona Jurema as he passed her, her laugh volcanic, her fat layered like lava. The younger woman, Eva, smiling happily, stood aside, looking even more Amazonian inside the house. They had crossed the scarred foyer, gone through a large, vomit-smelling dark ballroom turned into a tavern, and out the back door.

Coming again into the sunlight, each of the Tap Dancers

dropped his shorts and plunged into the swimming pool. With the encouragement of Dona Jurema and the smiles of Eva, Fletch had followed suit.

There were five white towels waiting for them when they came out of the pool. Their shorts had been piled neatly on a table near the back door.

The skinny young teenage girl brought them a tray with five glasses of cachaça and a sugar bowl.

Norival downed his cachaça in a gulp, asked for another, and collapsed on a long chair on the long side of the pool.

Tito was doing disciplined laps in the pool, stroking through the lily pads.

Orlando went into the house.

"What is that new North American verb?" Toninho asked. "Interact. It is tiresome having always to interact, especially with women. The women here do not expect anything so profound as interaction."

Dona Jurema came through the back door and let herself down the steps like a big bag of glass.

"So good of you to come, Toninho," she said. "Not many of the girls are up. Ah, it's a hot day. We had a busy night. We will have lunch for you in a while."

"This man." Toninho put his hands on Fletch's forearm. "This man has special needs."

Jurema beamed at Fletch. "It would be a sin if he is having difficulties."

"He is not having difficulties, I think," Toninho said. "Are you, Fletch?"

"Only with the cachaça." He put his glass down on the burned-out grass.

"A special need I'm sure you can satisfy, Jurema."

Arms akimbo, the woman shrugged her shoulders. It was a

seismic upheaval. "We can satisfy any need. Why, an Air Force General we had here—"

"Toninho," Fletch said. "I have no special needs."

"But you do," Toninho said. "A very special need. I am your friend. It is important to me that your special need be fulfilled."

"I need sleep," Fletch said, leaning back in his chair, closing his eyes.

"I know what you need." Solemnly, Toninho said, "My friend needs a corpse."

Fletch's eyes popped open. His head snapped up. "What?"

"I said you need a corpse. For the purpose of copulation." To Jurema, he said, "My friend has the great need to make love to a corpse."

Jurema was not laughing. She was answering Toninho in rapid Portuguese. Her eyes, her face, her voice bespoke someone doing business.

"Because," Toninho said, "my friend is a corpse. Partly a corpse. Part of him has not had a woman in forty-seven years. Clearly, if we are to get the truth from him, his perispirit must be awakened."

"Toninho!" Fletch said.

"It is true," Toninho said to Jurema.

Behind Fletch's long chair. Jurema bent over. She put her hands on his breasts and put at least part of her weight on them. Pressing hard, she ran her hands all the way down his stomach, under his towel to his pelvis, then raised her hands.

She erupted in laughter. "He seems alive. If the other part of him is as healthy …"

A cool breeze blew over Fletch. He resettled his towel.

"You see the problem," Toninho said with dignity. "Now. How can you help my friend?"

"Toninho. Stop it. You're gross."

"A corpse for my friend? Someone young, dead, and pretty."

"Toninho, this isn't funny."

"Probably by Tuesday," Jurema said. "There are always such corpses available during Carnival."

"Find a good one," Toninho said.

Jurema waddled a short distance. Speaking to Toninho in Portuguese, incredibly enough she stooped over and picked a weed out of the burned grass. Her face flushed. She then lifted herself up the back stairs and into the house.

"Tuesday," Toninho said. "She'll have one for you Tuesday."

"Toninho, I hope this is another of your jokes."

Abruptly, in the same tone of voice, Toninho said, "Your friend, Teodomiro da Costa, is to be respected."

"I met with him this morning." Fletch watched the sunlight flashing on Tito's shoulders as he swam. "He had advice for me, which I respect. Especially at the moment."

"In this country, seventy percent of the business is run by the government, you see. To do well on your own, as Teo has, is to do very well indeed. Now tell me. In North America, there is a car which has what is called a slant-six engine. Can you describe it to me, please?"

Fletch told Toninho what he understood of the slant-six engine, and that it had an especially long life. Sitting on Saturday morning in the mountains above Rio de Janeiro looking out into the sunlight, he felt his eyes crossing. He had not had that much of the cachaça. One moment Toninho was talking seriously of necrophilia and the next just as seriously about a slant-six car engine.

The young girl brought Norival his third cachaça.

"Ah," Toninho said. "Norival is an *arigó*. A simpleton, a boor, but a good fellow. If he were not from a rich, important family, he would be an *arigó*. His brother, Adroaldo Passarinho, is the same, exactly like him in every way. Look the same, act the same. His father has sent Adroaldo to school in Switzerland, in hopes there will be someone in the family this generation less than simple. *Arigó*."

Tito climbed out of the pool and, not drying himself, dropped naked belly down on the grass.

In high seriousness and in great detail, Toninho then wanted to know about this new robot he had read about in *Time* magazine supposedly capable of understanding and obeying one hundred thousand different orders. Designed in Milan, manufactured in Phoenix with Japanese parts. What was the nature of the computer which ran it? How were the joints designed, and how many were there? What would the robot say when given conflicting orders? Would the robot know, better than a person, when it is breaking down?

In his towel, holding a fresh glass of cachaça, Orlando stood on the back steps of the plantation house. He sang. Of the four Tap Dancers, Orlando's muscles were the heaviest. His voice was deep, and he sang well.

> *O canto de minha gente*
> *Assediando meu coração*
> *Semente que a arte germinou*
> *E o tempo temperou*
> *Amor, ô amor*
> *Como é gostoso amar*

Norival raised his head from his long chair and hissed. Even from a distance, it could be seen Norival was not focusing. His head dropped back.

"Ah, the *arigó* never sobered from last night," Toninho said.

"What's the song?" Fletch asked.

"An old Carnival song. Let's see." Toninho closed his eyes to translate. Fletch had been slow to see how long Toninho's lashes were. They rested on his cheeks. "'My people's song makes my heart leap. The seed is sown by art and tempered by time. Love, love, how good it is to love.'"

"That's a good song."

"Oh, yes."

With his glass of cachaça, Orlando wandered down to where they were sitting.

"Orlando," Toninho said. "Give Fletch a demonstration of capoeira, of kick-dancing. You and Tito. Make it good. Kill each other."

Raising his head beside the pool, Tito said, "You, Toninho."

"Perform for the gods," Toninho said.

Orlando looked into his glass. "I've had a drink."

"You won't hurt each other," Toninho said.

"You and Orlando," Tito said from the grass.

"It is important Janio sees capoeira from close up," Toninho said. "So he will remember."

Glass still in hand, Orlando went to Tito and with his bare feet stood on Tito's ass. Standing thus, he drained his glass, leaned over, and put it on the grass. Then he began to walk slowly up Tito's back.

"I can't breathe!" Tito said.

"And you can't talk?" Toninho asked.

"I can't talk, either."

Then he wriggled free, spilling Orlando to the side, and jumped to his feet.

In a wide arc, he swung his right foot, aiming for Orlando's head.

Orlando ducked successfully, turned sideways and slammed his instep into Tito's side, against his rib cage. Orlando's towel dropped.

"Wake up," Orlando said.

In a short moment, Tito and Orlando had the rhythm of it, had each other's rhythm. Gracefully, viciously, rhythmically, as if to the beating of drums, with fantastic speed they were aiming kicks at each other's heads, shoulders, stomachs, crotches, knees, each kick coming within a hair's breadth of connecting, narrowly ducking, sidestepping each other, turning and swirling, their legs straight and their legs bent, their muscles tight and their muscles loose, their fronts and their backs flashing in the sunlight, the hair on their heads seeming to have to hurry to keep up with this frantic movement. With this fast, graceful dance, easily they could have killed each other.

Eva had come onto the porch to watch. Her eyes flashed. A few faces of other women appeared in the upper windows of the plantation house. *Everyone loves the Tap Dancers ... They're sleek.*

"Remember ..." Toninho was saying. "A skill developed by the young male slaves, in defense against their masters. They would practice at night, to drums, so if their masters came down from the big house, to look for a woman, they could pretend to be dancing. Thanks to—what is the word in English?—miscegenation, such skills ultimately were not needed ..."

There was a loud *thwack!* and Tito began to fall sideways. He had taken a hard blow to the head from the instep of Orlando's foot. The blow could have been much, much harder. Tito did not fall completely.

"I told you to wake up," Orlando said regretfully.

Recovering, Tito charged Orlando like a bull, right into his midriff. Orlando fell backwards, Tito on top of him. Laughing, sweating, panting, they wrestled on the grass. At one point their bodies, their arms and legs, were in such a tight ball perhaps even they could not tell which was whose.

Eva, moving like time, went down to them.

Finally, Orlando was sitting on Tito and giving him pink-belly, pounding Tito's belly hard repeatedly with his fists. Tito was laughing so hard his stomach muscles were fully flexed and no harm was being done.

Standing over them, behind Orlando, Eva laced her fingers across Orlando's forehead and pulled him backward, and down.

Kneeling over Tito as he was, sitting on him, bent backward now so that his own back was on the ground, or on Tito's legs, Orlando looked up Eva's thighs. He rolled his eyes.

He jumped up and grabbed Eva by the hand.

Together Orlando and Eva ran down the grassy slope from the swimming pool and disappeared.

"You see?" Toninho said. "Uncomplicated."

After resting a moment on the ground, breathing hard, Tito rolled over and over and on into the pool of water.

"Your *Moby-Dick*," Toninho said abruptly. "By Herman Melville?"

Fletch looked at Toninho, wondering what new surprise was coming. "Yes," Fletch said. "I read it while waiting for a bus."

"'Call me Ishmael,'" Toninho quoted.

"Not a bad beginning," Fletch said. "Simple."

"Is it?" Toninho finished his cachaça. At the long side of the pool, Norival was finishing his fourth. "Is that Ishmael meant to be some spirit of the United States? Some guardian?"

"Almost anything can be said," Fletch said. "And has been."

"In a way, *Ismael* is the guiding spirit of Brazil."

Fletch said nothing. Necrophilia, slant-six car engines, the nature of *arigó*, robotics, capoeira, now a discussion regarding American literature.

"I'm quite certain Melville stopped in Brazil on his voyages. Have you even thought of that interpretation of *Moby-Dick*?"

"Melville meant Brazil is the guiding spirit of the United States?"

"Maybe of the hemisphere."

"Toninho ..." Tito's forearms were flat on the edge of the swimming pool, holding his head up. Water streamed down his face from his hair. His right ear was red from Orlando's kick. "I think we should do Norival a favor."

Toninho looked over at Norival stretched out in the sunlight. Norival bubble-belched. "Yes."

Toninho stood up.

Together Toninho and Tito tipped the slow-reacting Norival out of the long chair.

Fletch went to watch what new trick they would play.

Each taking an arm, they dragged Norival, belly down, to the bushes. The towel dragged off him in the dirt. Then, methodically, standing behind him, Toninho and Tito each picked up one of Norival's feet. They raised him so that his shins were on their shoulders.

Not all that gently, somewhat from the sides, they kicked Norival's soft, upside-down belly with the insteps of their feet, once, twice, some more.

"*Arigó*," Toninho said, kicking Norival's upside-down stomach.

"Empty out the sack," Tito said. "Very practical."

It didn't take too many kicks for Norival to begin vomiting his four cachaças, his numerous *chopinhos*, whatever was still in him from the night before.

Once he began vomiting, they dropped his legs on the ground.

Tito grinned at Fletch. "Very efficient, yes?"

"It seems to be working."

The other side of the swimming pool, Orlando and Eva were climbing back up the slope.

"Ah," Toninho said, watching them. "Five minutes is a long time in the life of such a mulatta."

Norival now was on his hands and knees, emptying himself into the bushes.

Bleary, drooling vomit, he looked up at them.

"*Obrigado*." In Portuguese, he said to them, "Thanks, guys."

13

After lunch, it rained.

The five young men sat in their muddy towels at a round table on the back porch of the old plantation house playing poker.

The humidity was complete, and even in the rain Fletch and Orlando and Tito had been in and out of the pool between hands. They would be either wet with sweat or wet with water, and the rain water, the pool water, seemed cooler. The only reason they sat under the roof to play was to keep the cards reasonably dry. Near them, their shorts were still piled on a small table, but the pile was messed up, as Norival had gone to his shorts and swallowed two pills from its pockets. They drank beer. There were many crushed cans near Norival's feet.

From under the porch roof, as he played, Fletch watched the rain fall on the pool and make mud puddles in the dead garden. He watched the flower-kissing birds sustain themselves with wings which beat so fast they were almost invisible, like auras on either side of their bodies, as they sucked sugar water from small vessels in the rafters.

Kick-dancing and flower-kissing birds.

After two or three hours of poker playing, it was clear who the winner was. Norival was careless, concerned more with his next *chope* than the cards. He seemed keyed-up anyway—for someone who had had so much to drink, even though properly evacuated before lunch. Fletch yawned. Tito, Orlando, and Toninho played cards in a way odd to Fletch. They did not seem to see the cards as they were, but as something else, something more. Always they believed in the next card too much. They believed in what the cards might be instead of what they were.

Fletch was collecting all the chips.

At one point, Toninho said, "Of course you cannot understand Brazil, Fletch. Three of us—all but Norival—have been to school in the United States. We cannot say we understand the United States, either. Everyone there is so anxious."

"Very nervous," Orlando said.

"Worried," Tito said. "Do I drink too much, smoke too much, make love too much, too little? Is my hair all right? Might someone see that my ankles are fat?"

"Does everyone *like* me?" Orlando guffawed.

"I'm so pretty!" Toninho said in falsetto. "Don't touch me!"

Fletch strummed the table with his fingers. "*Bum, bum, paticum bum, prugurundum.*"

The noise of the rain pounding on the tin roof increased.

Eva came through the back door and stood, watching them.

She stood behind Norival and watched his last chips disappear in careless play.

She took his feverish head in her hands and turned it sideways, and leaned his cheek against her bare stomach. "Ah, Norival," she said in Portuguese. "You are getting drunk again."

"*Arigó,*" Toninho said, clearly hoping for a picture card and playing as if he had one.

Eva rotated Norival's head so that he was slipping off

the chair. The front of his face was against her stomach. He breathed deeply a few times through his nose.

In a moment, Eva led Norival indoors.

Tito, Orlando, Fletch, and Toninho played silently.

Occasionally, concentrating, Toninho's lips would move as if he were talking, but no sound came out.

When Orlando won anything, no matter how much he had lost, his face would break into a marvelous grin. He would be ready to lose more.

At one point, when Fletch was raking in chips again, Tito murmured, "Your perispirit is with you."

"Is he telling you what cards we have?" Toninho asked.

"Doesn't need to," Fletch said. "I play with what I see I have against what I see you have."

From inside there was a short scream.

Toninho chuckled. "I guess Norival has a few surprises in him yet."

"We know he cannot hurt Eva," Tito said. "He is only a stick in her fire."

Then there was another, horrible, long drawn-out scream. It pierced the sound of the rain.

"They are playing," Orlando said.

"Norival!" Toninho called in Portuguese. "Mind your manners!"

Naked, Eva fell through the back door. "Norival!"

Her hair was messed up. Her eyes were wild.

She sucked in breath and spoke in a rush.

Toninho said, "She says Norival has stopped moving. That he has stopped breathing."

Eva was shouting Portuguese over the sound of the rain.

"He has passed out," Tito said.

"No." Alarmed, Toninho stood up. "She says he has stopped breathing!"

They all rushed inside.

More slowly, Fletch went with them, suspecting some new trick.

In the little room on the first floor, Norival lay on the rumpled, dirty sheets of an extra long bed. He was partly on his side, as if rolled into that position. He was naked and his stomach was slack. There was still a streak of mud on his leg.

Norival was grinning.

There was a happy, wicked gleam in his eye.

From the door, Fletch watched Norival's grin remain idiotic. Norival's eyes did not blink.

Fletch joined the Tap Dancers at the side of the bed. With his fingertips he felt for a pulse in Norival's neck. There was none. Norival's pleaded eyes did not blink.

As Fletch watched, slowly the grin disappeared from Norival's face. The lips became straight.

The happy gleam remained in his eyes.

A few inches in front of Norival's penis, the bed sheet was wet and stained.

"He is dead!" Orlando said in Portuguese.

Under his breath, Tito whistled.

Standing, his back straight, Toninho said, "Norival. You died *arigó.*"

"What do we do?" Orlando asked. "Norival is dead!"

"How did he die?" Tito asked. "Surely he has done this before. It hasn't been fatal."

Orlando said, "He can't be dead. Wake up, Norival! You'll miss Carnival!"

"He is dead," Toninho said. "Norival is dead!"

Eva filled the door of the small, dark room. Talking rapidly but more quietly now, she kept gasping, imitating a belch, grabbing her huge left breast with both hands.

"Died of a heart attack while copulating, I guess," Fletch said.

Orlando said, "Way to go, Norival!"

"No wonder he was smiling!" Tito said.

"You saw him smiling?" Toninho asked.

"Definitely he was smiling," Tito said.

Orlando nodded. "When we came into the room, he was smiling!"

"He is not smiling now," Tito said.

"But look at his eyes," Toninho said.

"His eyes are still happy," Tito said.

"And why not?" Orlando asked. "Why not happy?"

At the door, Eva was beginning to look pleased with herself.

"But he's dead!" Tito said.

"But how he died!" Orlando said. He looked ready to shake Norival's hand. "Well done, Norival!"

"A death in ten million," Toninho said. "*Arigó!*"

14

The tall, slim, naked young man stood in the dead garden, the rain pouring down his body, his feet wide apart in the mud, his face up to the rain, his arms held high as if to catch the sky.

From the back porch, Fletch heard what Toninho said to the sky:

> With God he lays down; with God he rises,
> With the grace of God and the Holy Spirit.
> May Thine eyes watch over him as he sleeps.
> Dead, will You light his way
> Into the mansions of eternity
> With the tapers of Thy Trinity?

Fletch went down to Toninho in the garden.

"A prayer." Toninho's face and arms lowered. His shoulders sagged.

Then Toninho looked over the hedges, out into mountain space in the rain. "Not a worry." Fletch could not make sure if there were tears mixed in with the rain on Toninho's cheeks. "When you die copulating, you are certain to come back to life, soon."

15

"Toninho! What do we do?" Tito asked in a hushed voice.

Toninho shook his head as if to clear it.

"Still, Norival is dead," he muttered thickly.

While Fletch and the Tap Dancers were out of the room, Dona Jurema, the young teenage girl, and one other woman from the house had washed Norival, put a fresher sheet under him, and laid him out straight.

Now in the small, dark room, Norival lay on his back, clean, naked. His eyes were closed. In his hands folded over his stomach were a few flowers which had seen better hours. A candle flickered at the head of the bed; another candle at the foot of the bed.

Leaving a full bottle of whiskey in the room, Dona Jurema left the young men sitting around the bed in straight wooden chairs.

So they had sat for two or three hours. The thick candles had burned down only a few centimeters.

There was no measurement tape on that whiskey bottle. Their next drink from it would probably be their last. Fletch had had three or four good swallows from the bottle.

Even on the straight wooden chair across the bed, Orlando sat with his legs out straight before him, his chin on his chest, his thumbs hitched into the tops of his shorts.

"We must do something," Tito said.

Toninho blinked.

"We cannot leave Norival here," Tito said.

To Fletch, Toninho said, "Norival comes from a rich, important family. His uncle is an admiral!"

"To die in a whorehouse," Tito said. "Full of booze …"

"And pills, I think," Fletch said.

"His mother would be disappointed," Tito concluded.

"But what a way to go!" Orlando muttered without opening his eyes or raising his chin from his chest.

"We must do something," Tito said.

"We must move him." Toninho drank from the bottle, saw that it was nearly the last of the whiskey, and handed the bottle to Tito.

"We must arrange some other death for Norival," Tito said.

"Burn the record," Fletch agreed. "I see the point."

"For the sake of his mother," Tito said.

"He must not have died here," Toninho said carefully. "Not in the arms of Eva."

"No," said Tito. "It would make her too famous."

"Still." Toninho winked. "People will know."

"Yes," Tito said. He passed the bottle over Norival to Fletch. "People will know how Norival died."

"What a way to go!" Orlando muttered.

"But not his mother," said Toninho.

"Not his mother," agreed Tito. "Not his sisters."

For a moment, while Fletch held the bottle, they were silent.

The candles flickered and Norival did not breathe.

Through the open window came the sound of the rain on the tin roof.

"We must do something," Tito said.

"The important thing is," Toninho said, trying very hard to keep his tongue straight and to see things clearly, "is to prevent an autopsy."

"Yes!" Tito said forcefully at this great wisdom.

"Because Norival was full of booze and pills."

"Despite our having emptied him out once," Tito put in.

"And that would disappoint his mother," said Toninho, losing his tongue in his mouth.

"Worth it," Orlando muttered from his chest. "A death in ten million. Good old Norival."

"Wake up, Orlando," Tito said. "We must think."

"No."

Toninho kicked Orlando's legs and Orlando nearly fell off his chair.

Blinking, he looked at Norival laid out on the bed, holding the wilted flowers.

It was not yet dark, but the rain made the candles bright in the small room.

"Orlando, we must think of something."

"*Queima de arquivo*," Fletch said. "I am learning Portuguese."

"Truly," Orlando said. "We must do something. We must move him."

"His boat," Toninho said.

"Yes." Orlando shook his head solemnly. "His boat. Who now will want his boat?"

"Exactly," Toninho said.

"Exactly what?" Tito asked.

Fletch took his drink from the bottle and handed it back across Norival to Orlando.

"Clearly." Toninho spoke slowly, carefully. "Norival died on his boat."

"Clearly." Tito looked at Norival as if for agreement. "Norival would have liked that."

Orlando said, "I think Norival was satisfied enough with the way he died."

"But we can say he died on his boat, Orlando," Tito said.

"Off his boat," Toninho corrected him. "He died off his boat. He drowned. That should prevent an autopsy."

"Yes," Tito said. "Poor Norival drowned. That should make his mother happy."

"You're all crazy," Fletch said.

"But Toninho," Tito asked, "how do we get Norival to his boat? It is way down in the harbor. There is a gate to the docks. Guards. There are always guards at the gate."

Again there was silence, as they considered the gate and guards leading to the dock where Norival's boat was.

Toninho took the bottle of whiskey from Orlando and finished it. "We walk him."

He placed the empty whiskey bottle on the bed, within Norival's reach.

Tito said something in Portuguese.

"We walk him right by the guards."

Orlando said, "This is a night the dead walk."

"Broomsticks." Toninho's eyes were now fully open. He was speaking perfectly clearly. "Jurema must have brooms."

Tito looked at the floor. "I sincerely doubt that, Toninho."

"Everyone has brooms. Tito, you get rope and rig a harness around Norival's chest. Under his arms. Orlando, you get brooms from Dona Jurema and saw them down to size. You know? So they will fit from the harness under his arms to his waist, so we can hold him up. We need some thick thread for his legs." Orlando and Tito were studying Toninho carefully with their eyes, putting all this together. Toninho jumped up. "There is a book of tide tables in the glove compartment of the car. I shall figure out exactly where Norival must drown to come ashore and be found in the morning."

"His wallet is in the car, too, Toninho," Tito said. "In the glove compartment. Norival must wear his wallet when he drowns, so when they find him in the morning, they will know who he is."

"Otherwise they will not report the body," Orlando said.

"They will report the body fast enough, if it's a Passarinho," Tito said. "Norival Passarinho."

"You help too, Fletch. You get Norival's clothes, including his shirt."

"You're all crazy," Fletch said. "What if we get caught with a corpse?"

Standing over Norival, Tito rubbed his own hands together. "Not a worry, Norival," he said. "We'll see that you died decently."

16

"Drive carefully, Toninho," Tito said. "We don't want an accident."

Although he was not going fast, Toninho was not being all that successful at keeping the black four-door Galaxie to the right. They were swerving down the wet, twisting mountainside road. It was now fully dark. A Volkswagen, climbing the road, had just blared its horn at them.

"We don't want to be stopped by the police," Orlando said.

"Drive as if you are driving a hearse," Tito advised.

"I am driving a hearse," Toninho said, swinging the wheel too much.

At Dona Jurema's, Orlando had sawed two broomsticks down to size. Tito bound Norival's chest with a rope harness. Toninho studied the tide tables and decided exactly where Norival was to drown in the South Atlantic Ocean. Together they fit the broomsticks into the harness and then dressed Norival.

While watching them carry Norival out of the old plantation house, Dona Jurema said to Fletch, "Come Tuesday. I'll have a corpse for you."

"Cancel the order," Fletch said. "We have a corpse."

Toninho sniffed. "Norival is not that sort of corpse."

As they swerved down the mountainside, Norival sat propped up in the backseat between Tito and Orlando. The broomsticks were not visible beneath his shirt.

When they came to the first flat, wide road on the outskirts of Rio de Janeiro, Tito reminded Toninho again to drive slowly, to stay to the right. Toninho drove very slowly. Even two children on roller skates passed them.

Toninho looked through the rearview mirror. "Norival never looked better. He holds his head up nicely."

The car swerved a little.

"Careful, Toninho," Tito clucked.

"The way he died, he should," Orlando said. "Not everybody—"

From behind them came the sound of a police siren.

"Oh, oh," Toninho said.

"Go fast, Toninho!" Tito said. "We have a corpse in the car!"

"No, no," Orlando said. "Stop."

The result of following these conflicting orders was that the car shot forward a few meters and then bucked to a stop.

On the backseat, Norival rolled forward. His head struck against the back of the front seat.

"Oh, Norival!" Tito said in exasperation.

"It's all right," Orlando said, pulling Norival back into a sitting position. "He won't bleed."

"Quick!" Toninho said. "Open his eyes! He looks more real that way!"

Orlando reached over with his fingers and opened Norival's eyes.

The police car drew alongside.

Apparently staring straight ahead through the windshield, Norival's eyes gleamed with a wicked joy.

"What did I do wrong?" Toninho asked. "These people have no respect for the dead!"

The conversation with the policeman of course was in Portuguese.

While it was going on, Fletch sat perfectly still in the front seat, trying not to look interested or concerned.

After they drove away from the policeman, Toninho, Orlando, and Tito, choking with laughter, repeated the conversation in English for Fletch.

Policeman: Why are you driving so slowly?

Toninho: It's Carnival, sir. I don't want to hit any revelers.

Policeman: No one else is driving so slowly.

Toninho: Perhaps no one else is as good a citizen as I, sir.

Policeman: Back there, you swerved. You almost hit a parked car.

Toninho: I sneezed.

Policeman: God bless you, my son.

Toninho: Thank you, sir.

Policeman: (shining his flashlight around the inside of the car, finally leaving it for a moment on Norival's joyfully beaming, unblinking face) Why does that guy look so happy?

Toninho: He always looks that way during
Carnival, sir.

Policeman: Is he stoned?

Toninho: (whispering) He's not all there, sir.

Policeman: Oh. Well, drive faster.

Toninho: Yes, sir.

* * *

"Tito, you stay with the car. Drive to where I showed you on the map. The beach. We'll be there in a few hours."

Correct. They had driven by the gates to the dock where Norival's boat was. The gates were closed and locked. Not one but three guards stood at the gate chatting, two outside and one inside.

They drove up the street and parked the car against the curb.

It had stopped raining. The moon was threatening to come out.

They lifted Norival out of the backseat and stood him in the road between Toninho and Orlando.

"Here, Fletch." Toninho handed Fletch a ball of heavy thread he had taken from Dona Jurema. "Tie Norival's left ankle to Orlando's right, his right ankle to my left. See? It will work out. That way, Norival will appear to walk."

Fletch tied Norival's left ankle to Orlando's right.

They lifted Norival a little off the ground on his broomsticks and Orlando walked in a circle around Toninho. Norival's movement was too slow.

"No, Fletch," Toninho said, "the line must be tighter. Norival must appear to be taking the same size steps as Orlando."

Kneeling on the wet road, Fletch retied the thread tighter, and then tied Norival's right ankle to Toninho's left.

Somewhere in the harbor, a ship's whistle blew.

Toninho and Orlando walked Norival up the road a little way. "How do we look, Tito?"

"Lift your side higher, Toninho," Tito said. "His foot is dragging a little, your side."

Toninho hitched Norival higher. "That better?"

"Perfect," Tito said. "You'd never know he's dead."

"Fine. Then we should go. See you at the beach in a few hours, Tito. Here, Fletch, you walk a little in front of us, in case things do not look exactly right."

Slowly, in bare feet, Fletch walked down the rain-slicked road and up onto the sidewalk toward the gate to the boat dock. Each pocket of his shorts was bulging with a wad of cruzeiros he had won at poker.

He could not help looking around.

Eyes beaming in complete joy, arms stiff at his sides, although his shoulders propped up by broomsticks did look a little high, Norival walked almost in step between Toninho and Orlando. Three close friends going down the street together. The harness kept Norival's head high.

Norival did trip going up the curb.

Down the road, Tito was driving the car away.

The three guards watched the four young men approach.

"*Boa noite*," Fletch said to them.

"*Boa noite*," they answered lowly, suspiciously.

Fletch stood aside.

"Ah, Doctor Passarinho!" One guard threw away his cigarette.

Again the conversation was in Portuguese.

Fletch kept looking up at the heavy, scudding clouds, hoping the moon would not take that moment to appear.

Guard: "You are not going out on your boat tonight, are you?"

Toninho answered in his normal voice, not even trying to conceal the movement of his lips. "Yes. Rio is so crowded. From Carnival. I need some peace and quiet."

Orlando took a few steps in his circle so that the faces of Norival and Toninho were turned a bit away from the guards.

Guard: "But there has been a heavy rain! It might rain again!"

Toninho/Norival: "That will help keep the sea calm."

Guard: "They say the wind will come up."

Toninho/Norival: "Yes, well, I feel like a vigorous sail."

Second guard: "You look uncommonly happy, Doctor Passarinho."

Toninho/Norival: "I think I have met the love of my life."

Guard: "That will do it."

Toninho/Norival: "Yes. I doubt I will ever love anyone else."

Third guard: (inside gate) "Ah, to be in love! To be young and in love! You look so happy, Doctor Passarinho!"

Guard: "But if you go sailing now, you will be missing the parties! The grand balls! How can there be Carnival parties without the Tap Dancers?"

Orlando: "No. Only Norival is going sailing. Because he is so stuck in love, you see. We came just to see him off. We will swim ashore. Off Copacabana."

Second guard: "I understand everything perfectly. He is in love … From the stiff way he walks, I should say he should not be with the young lady just now …"

Guard: "Is that it? Ah! I see! So Doctor Passarinho, even though it is the middle of the night during Carnival, goes sailing!"

Third guard: "What a man!"

Guard: "What a gentleman!"

Toninho/Norival: "Something like that."

Guard: "Norival Passarinho must do what is best, for himself and his young lady!" He signaled the guard inside to open the gate. "What consideration!"

Orlando and Toninho marched Norival through the gate. True, Norival did walk as if he suffered one of the more virulent social diseases.

Fletch fell in behind them.

Toninho/Norival: "*Obrigado! Boa noite!*"

ABOARD, Orlando removed the sail covers and had the mainsail up in almost no time at all.

Toninho released the bow line and gathered it in.

As soon as the mainsail caught wind, Fletch, at the tiller, released the stern line and, letting it trail in the water, took in the main sheet.

Facing aft in the cockpit, Norival beamed delightedly at his friends taking him sailing.

While Orlando was running up the jib, Toninho came aft and took the tiller. "I know the harbor," he said. "We do not want to run into someone's boat in the dark while one of us is dead."

Fletch gathered in the stern line. "Not in the S. S. *Coitus Interruptus.*"

The moon came out.

In the moonlight, Norival's whole face beamed. But when the boat heeled, he fell over sideways.

"Can't have him rolling around," Toninho said. "He might go overboard before we mean him to."

Fletch relieved Norival of his rope harness and the broomsticks and sat him up in the leeward corner of the cockpit. He tied a light line around his shoulders to a stanchion behind him.

"The things we do for our friends," Toninho muttered, coming about.

Now Norival was sitting to windward, leaning unnaturally forward as if being seasick. But he was still beaming.

Orlando joined them in the cockpit.

Laughing, then, they translated the conversation with the guards for Fletch. "*What a gentleman!*" Orlando kept repeating.

Then Orlando said, "Norival loved this little boat."

At the tiller, Toninho said, "Who'd think Norival would be one to go down with his ship?"

Orlando laughed. "What a gentleman!"

"We're just about there," Toninho said.

Ashore, as they came around a point, a car's headlights went on and off three times.

"Yes!" Toninho said. "There's Tito. He must see us."

At first, sailing south in Baia de Guanabara, Fletch had tried to sleep. He lay on the deck, a cushion under his head. He regretted leaving the rest of his mineral water in the car. Despite the drinks he had had, sleep was impossible.

The sky was clear now. The breeze was from the northeast and steady. The little sloop moved nicely through the water.

To starboard, Cidade Maravilhosa, Rio de Janeiro, passed slowly, laid out under the moonlight. There were a few fires on the beach. The street lights, the lights in the tall apartment buildings and hotels along the shore dimmed the stars above. From offshore, the samba drums were heard from all parts of the city in a soft jumble. Like no other city Fletch had seen from such a perspective, Rio has peculiar black holes in its middle, the sides of its cliffs, *Morro da Babilônia, de São João, des Cabritos, Pedra dos, Dois Irmãos*, its surprising, irrepressible jungle growth within the city. Above all in the moonlight, arms out in forgiveness, stood the statue of Christ the Redeemer.

At some point, sitting in the cockpit opposite Norival, Orlando had said, "We will have to go to Canecão Ball."

"Yes," Toninho said. "However late."

"We will have to find the Passarinhos," Orlando said, "and say that Norival went sailing."

"Janio, you must stay with us so we will be believed."

"I should return to the Yellow Parrot."

"No, no. There will not be time. You come to my apartment. You can wear my costume from last year. We are the same size."

"I seem to be the same size as everybody," Fletch said. "Alan Stanwyk, Janio Barreto, Toninho Braga …"

"Tito will drive fast and we will dress and go in a hurry."

"The tickets Teo gave me for the ball are at the Yellow Parrot."

"You can use Norival's. He won't be needing it."

They sailed another few kilometers. Ashore, again Tito flashed his headlights three times.

"All right." Toninho punched Fletch's leg. "Take the tiller, Senhor Barreto. It is no surprise to us you know how to run a boat. Orlando, assist Norival. Make sure he has his wallet in his pocket."

"He has his wallet."

"His death would never be reported, unless they know who he is. Whoever finds a Passarinho body will expect money for reporting it."

Fletch sat, tiller in hand, keeping the course along the shore.

Toninho went below.

Soon from the small cabin came a heavy pounding. Then a splintering sound. Then gurgling.

The boat veered to port. Instantly, it became unmanageable. The sails luffed.

Fletch released the tiller.

Toninho came up the companionway and tossed a hammer overboard.

"We are near enough the rock for people to believe he hit it," Toninho said. "And now for Norival."

Together, Toninho and Orlando lifted Norival, his eyes still beaming happily in the moonlight, brought him to the gunwale. Gently, they dropped him overboard.

For a moment, the two young men stood on the deck, staring down into the water. Toninho's lips moved. Orlando crossed himself.

"He'll be on the beach by dawn," Toninho said.

The little boat first had come about, put its nose up into the wind, both sails luffing. Then the bow began to sink. As it did so, it fell off the wind, the sails filled again, and, twisting, it began to capsize.

"Come, Janio!" Toninho shouted. "You don't want to keep dying at your age!"

Orlando dove overboard.

Only after Fletch dove did Toninho scramble off the sinking boat.

The water was exactly body temperature, as was the air. In irrepressible, sensuous delight, Fletch stroked through the buoyant water toward Cidade Maravilhosa.

The wads of money in the pockets of his shorts came to feel like stones in the water.

After a hundred meters, he stopped swimming. He looked around to see if anything of the boat was still visible. He could not be sure. There was something white on the water, possibly the side of the hull, possibly the sails.

Then, from near the boat came a loud yell. "*Aaaaaaaaarrrrrgh!*" Water was thrashed.

"Toninho!" Fletch called. "What's the matter?"

Silence.

"Toninho! What happened?"

Fletch was just starting to swim back when Toninho's steady voice came calmly across the water surface: "I swam into Norival ..."

17

"We must be very casual," said Tito, now a movie Indian.

They were entering the Canecão Night Club.

"What is the number of the Passarinho box?" Orlando asked.

"They're always in box three," Toninho answered.

"Da Costa is in box nine," Fletch answered.

Relieved of the corpse, Tito drove the black four-door Galaxie back to Copacabana fast enough to satisfy any police.

In the car, Fletch gulped down the rest of his liter of water.

At Toninho's apartment on Rua Figueiredo Magalhaes, Toninho, Tito, Orlando, and Fletch shaved and showered in assembly-line fashion.

The Tap Dancers were to dress as movie Indians in breechclouts, soft thigh-high boots, and war paint. Norival's breechclout did not fit Fletch, unless he wanted to spend the rest of the night holding it up with his hand.

Toninho dug his last year's costume out of a closet and tossed it to Fletch: a one-piece shiny satin movie cowboy suit, complete with mask, frayed leggings, and spangles. Fletch wriggled into it.

"Toninho. This is a scuba suit?"

"It fits you perfectly. Here are the boots, the hat, the mask."

"It fits like a scuba suit."

Toninho, Tito, and Orlando then sat in a circle decorating each other's faces, chests, backs with movie war paint, with great speed. Finished, they looked as if they had already sweated through a war.

While they were doing that, Fletch decorated Toninho's apartment by draping wet cruzeiros every conceivable place to dry.

"Remember," Tito said. "Very casual."

At Canecão Night Club, Orlando opened the door to the Passarinho box.

"Orlando!" people exclaimed. "Tito! Toninho!"

The people in the box just stared at the masked movie cowboy.

Below them, the huge floor of the Canecão Night Club was jammed with people in bright costumes at little tables, on the dance floor, wandering around. Across the hall on the large stage was an enormous band, mostly of samba drums, but of horns and electric guitars as well.

Everyone in the Passarinho box made much of the Tap Dancers' costumes. As there wasn't much to the costumes, in fact they were making much of the Tap Dancers.

In turn, Toninho, Orlando, and Tito exercised the courtesy of not knowing who people were and expressing great surprise when, for example, Harlequin revealed himself to be Admiral Passarinho.

"You're very late!"

"Oh," Toninho equivocated. "We just found the box."

"Who's this?" a woman asked.

"Janio Barreto," Toninho muttered.

"I. M. Fletcher."

Senhor Passarinho was dressed as Papai Noel. "Where's Norival?"

"He went sailing," Tito said.

"Sailing? It is storming out!"

"The storm is over," Orlando said.

"Sailing? On the night of the Canecão Ball?"

"We saw him off," Toninho said. "Fletch did too."

"Sailing? Why would he go sailing the night of the Canecão Ball?"

With apparent concern, Toninho said, "Norival has been acting very serious lately."

"He has been talking of taking up a career," Orlando said.

"That would be nice," said Papai Noel.

"It is a question of what he does best," Tito said.

"Norival has his talents," Orlando said.

Toninho said, "Perhaps he wanted to think."

"Norival becoming serious?" asked Harlequin. "Then it is time for me to retire!"

"No, no," Toninho said. "You don't know Norival as we do. When Norival sets his mind to something, he is apt to die trying."

"Norival can be very sincere," Orlando said. "About some things."

"Yes." Accented by war paint, Toninho's eyes crossed. "Norival is one to die trying."

"Norival is not coming to the ball at all?" Harlequin asked.

"He went sailing," Toninho said lamely. "To come to some conclusion ..."

"Ah, what a son!" Papai Noel said. "Probably drunk somewhere! These tickets cost three hundred North American dollars each! Norival, Adroaldo ... Why does a man have sons? As soon as they grow as big as he is, they ignore him! They take, but do not give!"

Fletch was introduced to Senhora Passarinho, who sat aside,

watching the dancers on the floor. A lady with mild, vague eyes, she was dressed as a circus clown.

"Ah!" she said. "Norival went sailing! Of course, he never was one for parties! A quiet, sensitive boy, always. He wrote poetry, you know, when he was younger. I remember one poem of his, where the cockatoo bird was meant to represent his school principal ..."

"You see," Tito said aside to Fletch. "We could not disappoint that lady with the truth."

"Clearly."

"It would kill her."

"Have a drink!" ordered Harlequin. "Cachaça?"

Toninho grinned broadly. The worst was over. "*Nao, Senhor.* We must go find girls."

"Of course you must!" boomed Papai Noel. "The night is as young as you!"

"Just make sure they're not men disguised surgically!" Harlequin warned.

"If I find someone special, I shall bring her to you," Toninho said, "to check out."

Harlequin roared in laughter.

Outside the box, Fletch said, "Toninho, are you going back to the beach in the morning to make sure Norival came ashore?"

"Oh, no." Toninho adjusted the top of his boot against the bare calf of his leg. "Today is Sunday. We must go to mass."

TEODOMIRO DA COSTA was standing at the little bar at the back of his box.

"Who is this?" he exclaimed. "I don't recognize you!"

Fletch stared at him the appropriate time through his mask.

Everyone else in the box was facing forward, listening intently to the singer of the moment.

What was left of the Tap Dancers had gone looking for girls.

"You scare me, Senhor Gunslinger! What do you want?"

"It's me, Teo."

"Who?" Teo leaned forward, staring through the eyeholes of Fletch's mask.

"Fletch!"

"Ah!" Teo feigned a look of great relief. "Then come have a drink."

The barman Teo had brought from his house began to make Fletch a screwdriver.

"It's so late," Teo said. "It is nearly three o'clock in the morning. Did you fall asleep?"

"No."

"I thought not."

"Without Laura, I went for a tour of the suburbs. Got back late."

"In a bus?"

"Something like that. A big car."

The singer stopped singing.

"Oh, Fletch! Beautiful costume!" the Viana woman said. "Where did you get it?"

"I mugged someone on my television set."

"It fits you ..." She looked below his waist. "... handsomely."

"Frankly, I feel like I'm walking behind myself."

"You are, darling. You are."

Teo introduced Fletch to his other guests. Besides the Vianas and the da Silvas, there was a famous Brazilian soccer player who could not stop dancing around the box by himself; his wife, who was taller than he, and probably heavier; a broker and his wife from London, who put on their Wegman—Man Ray masks for Fletch; Adrian Fawcett, who wrote about music for the *New York Times*; an Italian racing car driver and his girlfriend, who was very young indeed; and the young French film star Jetta.

Everyone marveled at Fletch's costume, and he at everyone's. Teo was dressed somewhat as a tiger, with a short tail. His tiger head rested on the bar table. Staring unblinkingly through glass eyes, the tiger head reminded Fletch somewhat of Norival in his last moment. But Norival's eyes were much happier.

Jetta was dressed in a nurse's cap and costume, white shoes. Her nurse's skirt was not even as long as the Tap Dancers' breechclouts.

In films, he had seen more of Jetta.

Fletch took off his mask and movie cowboy hat and stood at the rail and watched the swirl of color and flesh below him.

A few of the drummers were going off the stage; others were coming on. The music would never stop.

At three places on the huge floor, between the dancing area and the tables, were tall, raised, gilded cages. Inside, three or four magnificent women dressed only in G-strings and tall headgear writhed to the music. Outside, crawling around the cages, trying to attain sufficient footholds in their high-heeled shoes to writhe to the music, nine or ten women dressed in G-strings and tall headgear crawled around like big cats on their hind legs. Each of the gilded cages was a locus of writhing brown bare asses and huge, shaking brown bare breasts.

Beside him, Teo said, "The floors of the cages are elevators; they go up and down so the women can get in and out without being accosted by the crowd."

"They must be seven feet tall," Fletch said.

"They are all over six feet."

"What about the women outside the cages?"

"They were not women." Teo sipped his drink.

"They are."

Teo said, "They are exhibiting the superb work of their Brazilian surgeons."

From a distance, Fletch could see no difference between the women inside the cages and the women outside the cages.

Once before, in New York, he had been fooled.

"No one hardly ever accosts them," Teo said. "Very sad, for them."

The music picked up, and all the people, those dancing, those at the tables, those in the boxes, began singing/chanting the song presented by Império Serrano that Carnival. Fletch stumbled over the lyrics. He could never make his Portuguese sibilant enough.

All the tanned people, the brown people, the black people were moving to the rhythm and singing the lyrics of the song presented by a single samba school together, something about how indebted Brazilian people are to the coffee bean, and how they should respect the coffee bean like an uncle.

Adrian Fawcett, drink in hand, stood at the rail to Fletch's left. "Brazil is what the United States would like to think it is."

"I used to work for a newspaper," Fletch said. "A reporter."

"What do you do now?"

"Do? Why must I do? I am."

Jetta stood the other side of Fletch. After Eva, after watching the women in the gilded cages, Jetta-off-the-screen seemed small.

"Really what do you do?" Adrian asked.

Fletch said, "I don't know."

Jetta said, "Teo said there would be someone young for me to dance with."

"I feel one hundred years old at the moment."

"I have heard that story," she said. "You are someone who died, years ago, murdered, and has come back to life to reveal your murderer."

"Did you ever hear anything so crazy?"

"Yes," she said. "Will you dance?"

Fletch wanted to crawl into a corner of the box, to sleep. He was sure he could do so, despite the drums, the horns, the guitars, the singing. "Of course."

Excusing themselves from the box, they went to the dance floor.

The people swirling around them were dressed as rabbits and rodents, harlequins and harlots, grande dames and play school children, villains and viscounts, convicts and cooks, pirates and priests.

Surprising to Fletch, Jetta seemed a wooden dancer. She clung to Fletch as she might to a log in the middle of the sea. He suspected she resisted such music.

A few meters away, Orlando, breechclout flapping, was dancing wildly with a woman in a blond wig. The concentration in his eyes as he danced put him in another world. The woman's dress exposed only one breast totally.

At the edge of the dance floor, a dozen men stood absolutely still, staring up, their mouths agape. Above them was a woman sitting on the rail of a box, her bare buttocks hanging over the rail. The woman herself was not visible: just her bare buttocks hanging over the rail.

Jetta followed Fletch's gaze. "Brazilians are so relaxed about their bodies," said the young French film star. "So practical."

Feeling almost intoxicated with sleeplessness, Fletch envisioned Tito and Toninho turning Norival upside down in the bushes, kicking the vomit out of his stomach; Tito and Orlando, naked, kick-dancing, then wrestling, laughing, on the burned-out grass; the magnificent Eva standing in the door of the small, dark room where Norival lay dead, clutching her left breast with both hands, looking mildly pleased with herself; harness and broomsticks and calculating where a corpse dropped into the tide would be by dawn ...

Jetta ran her hands up the smooth sleeves of Fletch's shirt to his shoulders and said, "You were so late in coming."

Even though dancing, sleep passed through Fletch's brain like a curtain dragging across a stage. "I had to sit up a sick friend."

18

Alone in his room at the Hotel Yellow Parrot, Fletch first dialed the Hotel Jangada and asked for Room 912.

There was no answer in Room 912.

Not even taking off his movie cowboy suit, he fell on his bed. He thought he would sleep immediately. It was nearly seven o'clock in the morning. He was not used to going to sleep at seven o'clock in the morning.

Getting up, he dropped his clothes on the floor. Then he crawled beneath the sheet.

Even at that hour of the bright morning, the sound of a samba combo could be heard from somewhere in the street. He rolled onto his side and pulled the pillow over his ear. Eyes closed, flesh wavered everywhere in his mind: big, soft, pliant breasts with huge nipples swinging to the beat; long, smooth backs danced away from him; brown buttocks dimpled as they moved; gorgeous long legs bent and straightened as feet pressed gently against the earth, the dance floor in the rhythm of the melodic samba drums.

Fletch got out of bed and called room service for breakfast.

While he waited, he took a long, hot shower.

Alone, a towel around his waist, he ate breakfast sitting in a corner of his room. Sunday morning. For once, the man across the utility area was not painting the room.

He called the Hotel Jangada again, again asked for Mrs. Joan Stanwyk in Room 912.

Again there was no answer.

He closed the drapes against the bright morning and got into bed.

He tried lying like a statue on a crypt, like Norival dead on the bed at the old plantation house, flat on his back, his hands crossed on his stomach. He tried counting the members of a woman's pole-vaulting team leaping over the barrier. At the nineteenth redhead taking her turn with the brunettes and blonds going over the barrier, he knew sleep was unattainable.

He called the Hotel Jangada again.

Heavily slogging around the room, he opened the window drapes.

He pulled on clean shorts, a clean tennis shirt, socks, and sneakers.

Outside the hotel, in the brilliant sunlight, the small boy, Idalina's great-grandson Janio Barreto, was waiting for him.

The boy grabbed Fletch's arm. He hobbled along with Fletch, speaking rapidly, softly, insistently.

Fletch shook the boy off and got into his MP.

On his wooden leg, the ten-year-old Janio Barreto ran after Fletch's car, calling to him.

19

"*Bom dia*," Fletch said to the formally dressed desk clerk at the Hotel Jangada. "There is a problem."

Instantly, the man was solicitous. He put his forearms on the reception counter and folded his hands. "Are you a guest of this hotel?"

"I am staying at the Hotel Yellow Parrot."

The desk clerk was only a little less solicitous. The Hotel Yellow Parrot was a good hotel, too, more traditional, not so flashy. All the good hotels in Rio de Janeiro exactly doubled their rates during Carnival.

Fletch had already telephoned Room 912 on the house phone, gone to the door, checked out the breakfast and pool areas. No sign of Joan Collins Stanwyk. The note he had left for her was still in the Room 912 box behind the reception desk.

He spoke slowly and distinctly: "Someone who is staying at your hotel, a North American woman named Mrs. Joan Stanwyk, talked to me yesterday morning at about this time, at my hotel. We arranged to meet almost immediately here, for breakfast. She was to walk from there to here. All I had to do was to get something from the safe of the Hotel Yellow Parrot, shower, change clothes (I had been jogging), and follow her in my car. I left the Hotel Yellow Parrot about a half hour after her, and drove straight here. She did not answer the house phone. She did not answer when I knocked on her door. She was not in the breakfast room, the terraces, the swimming pool areas, the bar. She still doesn't answer. I'm afraid something must have happened to her."

The desk clerk smiled faintly at this story of a jilted lover. "There is nothing we can do, Senhor. We must respect the privacy of our guests. If the lady does not wish to see you, or hear from you …" Raising his hands from the counter, he shrugged.

"But, you see, she needs something from me. Money. She had been robbed of everything."

Again the man shrugged.

"I left her a note." Fletch pointed to the note still in its slot behind the man. "The note is still there."

"People change their plans rapidly in Rio during Carnival." The man smiled. "Sometimes they change their whole characters."

"Will you let me into her room, please?" Fletch had already tried to jimmy the lock to Room 912. It was an advanced lock, designed for only the most advanced burglars. "I worry that something must have happened to her. She may need help."

"No, sir. We cannot do that." "Will you go yourself?"

"No, sir. I cannot do that."

"Will you send a maid in?"

"It's Carnival." The desk clerk looked at the lobby clock. "It is early. People sleep odd hours. They do not want disturbance."

"She's been missing twenty-four hours," Fletch said. "It is now a police matter."

The man shrugged.

Fletch said, "*Onde é a delegacia?*"

"IS THERE A POLICE OFFICER WHO SPEAKS ENGLISH?"

"Spik Onglish," the police officer behind the tall desk said. "Quack, quack."

Fletch turned his head so a younger police officer down the counter could hear him. "Anyone here who can speak English?"

Down the counter, the younger officer picked up a phone, dialed a short number, and spoke into it.

After he hung up, he held the palm of his hand up to Fletch, either ordering him to stop or suggesting he wait.

Fletch waited.

The lobby of the police station was filled with regretful revelers. On the floor and along the bench sat and lay men and women of all shapes, sizes, colors, in nearly every state of dress and undress, sleeping, trying to sleep, blinking slowly, holding their heads. Some of the revelers were in Carnival costumes, now in tatters: a queen; a mouse; ironically, a magistrate. One hairy man, asleep with his mouth open, was dressed only in bra, panties, and garter belts. A fat woman, eating cookies from a bag, was dressed as the Queen of Sheba. Five or six of the men had cuts and bruises on their heads; one had a nasty long cut down the calf of his leg. Even with no glass in the windows, the room smelled putrid.

While Fletch waited, a man dressed only in tank trunks entered. A long-handled knife stuck into the area between his chest and his shoulder. He walked perfectly well. With dignity, he said to the police officer at the high counter, "*Perdi minha máquina fotográfica.*"

From the bottom of a flight of stone stairs, a heavy police officer beckoned Fletch to come to him.

"My name is Fletcher."

The man shook hands with him. "Barbosa," the man said, "Sergeant Paulo Barbosa. Are you North American?"

"Yes, sir."

The sergeant heavily led Fletch up the stairs. "I have been to the United States. To New Bedford, Massachusetts." He led Fletch into a little room with a desk and two chairs. The sergeant sat in the chair behind the desk. "I have cousins there, in New Bedford, Massachusetts." He lit a cigarette. "Have you been to New Bedford, Massachusetts?"

"No." Fletch sat down.

"It is very nice in New Bedford, Massachusetts. Very sealike. It is on the sea. Everyone there fishes. Everyone's wife runs a gift shop. My cousin's wife runs a gift shop. My cousin fishes." The sergeant brushed cigarette ashes from his shirt when there were no cigarette ashes on his shirt. "I truly believe the Portuguese bread is better in New Bedford, Massachusetts than the Portuguese bread in Rio de Janeiro. Some of it. Ah, yes. New Bedford, Massachusetts. I was there almost a year. I helped my cousin fish. Too cold there. I could not stand the cold."

The man sat sideways to the desk, not looking at Fletch. "Are you enjoying Carnival?"

"Very much."

"Ah, to be young, handsome, healthy in Rio during Carnival! Can you come closer to heaven? I remember." Then he brushed cigarette ashes off his shirt which were truly there. "And rich, too, I suppose."

In a corner of the room behind the desk was a gray steel filing cabinet, with three drawers.

"It must be a busy time for the police."

"It is," the sergeant agreed. "We get to enjoy Carnival very little. Everything goes topsy-turvy, you see." He smiled at Fletch, slyly proud of this idiom. "Topsy-turvy. Men become women; women become men; grown-ups become children; children become grown-ups; rich people pretend they're poor; poor people, rich; sober people become drunkards; thieves become generous. Very topsy-turvy."

Fletch's eyes examined the typewriter on the desk. It was a Remington, perhaps seventy-five years old.

"You were robbed ..." the sergeant guessed.

"No," Fletch said.

"You were not robbed?"

"Of course I was robbed," Fletch said. "When I first came here." The sergeant seemed to be relieved. "But I am not bothering you with such a small, personal matter."

The man smiled happily, in increased respect for Fletch. He turned and faced Fletch, now ready to listen.

Again, slowly, carefully, Fletch told Sergeant Paulo Barbosa the facts of his meeting Joan Collins Stanwyk at the Hotel Yellow Parrot, arranging to bring money to the Hotel Jangada, as of course she had been robbed, to have breakfast with her ... her not being at the hotel yesterday or today ... not picking up the note he had left for her ...

Another cigarette was dropping ashes on the sergeant's shirt. He was quick to brush them away.

"Ah," he said, "Carnival! It explains everything."

"This is not a crazy lady," Fletch said. "She is a woman of many responsibilities. She is a healthy, attractive blond woman in her early thirties, expensively dressed—"

"Topsy-turvy," the sergeant said. "If you say she is not a crazy lady, then during Carnival, she becomes a crazy lady! I know! I have been on this police force twenty-seven years. Twenty-seven Carnivals!"

"She has been missing for over twenty-four hours."

"Some people go missing all their lives! They come to Brazil because they go missing from some place else. Don't you know that?"

"Not this lady. She has a magnificent home in California, a daughter. She is a wealthy woman."

"Ah, people during Carnival!" The sergeant puffed on his cigarette philosophically. "They are apt to do anything!"

"She could be kidnapped, mugged, hurt, run over by a taxi."

"That is true," the sergeant said. "She could be."

"It is very important that we find her."

"Find her?" The sergeant seemed truly surprised at the suggestion. "Find her? This is a huge country! A city of nine million people! Tall buildings, short buildings, mountains, tunnels, parks, jungles! Are we supposed to look on top of every tall building and under every short building?" He sat forward in his chair. "At this time of year, everyone becomes someone else. Everyone wears a mask! There are people dressed as goats out there! As porpoises! Tell me, are we to look for a goat, or a porpoise?"

"For a blonde, trim North American woman in her early thirties ..."

"Topsy-turvy!" the sergeant exclaimed. "Be reasonable! What can we do?"

"I am reporting the disappearance of a female North American visitor to Brazil—"

"You've reported it! If she walks into the police station, I'll tell her you're looking for her!"

"I don't see you taking notes," Fletch said firmly. "I don't see you making up a report."

The sergeant's eyes grew round in amazement. "You want me to type up a report?"

"I would expect that, yes."

"I should type up a report because some North American woman changed her plans?"

"A report should be filed," Fletch insisted. "Any police force in the world—"

"All right!" The sergeant opened his desk drawer." I'll type up a report! Just as you say!" He took a key from his desk. "You want me to type up a report, I'll type up a report!" Standing, he went to the filing cabinet and inserted the key into its lock. First he looked in the top drawer, then the middle drawer. "Anything to keep the tourists happy!"

From the bottom drawer, he took out a typewriter ribbon. It appeared to be just about as old as the typewriter.

The sergeant blew dust off the typewriter ribbon.

"Never mind." Fletch stood up." I get the point."

From a telephone kiosk on the sidewalk outside the police station, Fletch called Teodomiro da Costa.

Teo answered the phone himself.

"Teo? Fletch. I knew if you were asleep, your houseman would tell me."

"I have to wait for some Telexes from Japan. I am preparing to sell some yen."

"Teo, that woman I mentioned to you yesterday morning, the North American, is still missing. The note I left for her at the Hotel Jangada has not been picked up. She has no money, no identification. I have been to the police. They tell me there is nothing they can do. The people at the Hotel Jangada will not let me into her room. She may be very sick, Teo, or—"

"Of course. I understand. I think the first thing is to inspect her room. She was a healthy woman, you say?"

"Very healthy. Very sensible."

"Where are you now?"

"Outside the police station."

"I'll meet you at the Hotel Jangada."

"Teo, you've been awake all night."

"That's all right. This could be a very serious matter, Fletch. Just let these Telexes arrive, and I will be right there."

"Thanks, Teo. I'll wait in the bar."

20

"What is the woman's name?"

"Joan Collins Stanwyk," Fletch answered. "Room nine-twelve."

Fletch was on his second guarana when Teo appeared in the door of the bar of the Hotel Jangada. Even in shorts and a tennis shirt, the dignity of Teodomiro da Costa was absolute.

At the reception counter, Teo spoke with the same clerk with whom Fletch had spoken.

Fletch stood aside and listened.

Clearly, in Portuguese, Teodomiro da Costa introduced himself, explained the situation as he knew it and stated his request: that they be permitted to inspect Room 912.

Again, with all apparent courtesy, the desk clerk refused.

The conversation became more rapid. Teo said something; the desk clerk said something; Teo said something, smiling politely; the desk clerk said something.

Finally, drawing himself up, giving the desk clerk his hooded eye, Teodomiro da Costa asked the rhetorical question which is magic in Brazil, which opens all doors, closes all doors, causes things to happen—or not happen, according to the speaker's wish—which puts people in their places: "*Sabe com quem está falando?:* Do you realize to whom you are speaking?"

The desk clerk withered.

He got the desk key to Room 912 and led the way to the elevator.

"Do you see anything amiss?" Teo asked.

While the desk clerk stood at the door of Suite 912, jangling the key in his hand, Teo and Fletch had searched through the living room, bedroom, bathroom, terrace as well as they could.

"Not a damned thing," Fletch answered. "Except that Joan Collins Stanwyk isn't here."

The rooms were freshly made up, the bathroom undisturbed, the bed not slept in. Going through the drawers, closets, even going through the medicine chest and suitcases, and other immediately conceivable hiding places, Fletch had found no money, no jewelry.

"One thing is significant, Teo," Fletch said. "Yesterday morning, Joan was wearing a tan slacks suit and a silk shirt. I cannot find the slacks suit and the shirt here in the suite."

"She could have sent them to the hotel cleaners. You don't know what other clothes she had."

"Not likely. She wanted to move out of this hotel as soon as I brought money."

"Then it is likely she disappeared somewhere between the Hotel Yellow Parrot and here."

"Yes."

Standing back on his heels at the door, the desk clerk rattled the key against its chain.

"What do we do now?" Teo asked. "You're the investigative reporter, newly retired."

"Check the hospitals, I guess."

Teo thought a short moment. "There is really only one hospital where they would have brought anyone sick or injured between the Yellow Parrot and here. We can check that one out."

Fletch said, "Let's do so."

"WHAT DO WE DO NOW?" Teo asked again.

They stood in the hospital lobby.

Teo had explained to the hospital administrator the disappearance of a blonde North American woman, in good health, more than twenty-four hours before, who had already been robbed of her money and identification.

The administrator clucked about Carnival, was most understanding although not alarmed, and permitted Teo and Fletch to walk through the seven floors of the hospital, checking the beds of every reasonable unit.

The administrator had said there were many people without identification in the hospital during Carnival. She would be grateful to have any of them identified.

"I don't know." Fletch's eyes wanted to close in sleep, in discouragement, perhaps to think.

"I don't see what else we can do," Teo said.

"Neither do I."

"Once in a while you have to let time pass …" Teo said.

"I guess so."

"Let things right themselves."

"She could be anywhere," Fletch said. "Anything could have happened to her. Should I check all the hospitals in Rio?"

"That would be impossible! Then check all the hotels and hospitals and jails in Brazil, one by one? You can't live so old!"

"I guess not."

"Let time pass, Fletch."

"Thank you, Teo. Sorry to keep you up."

"You have done your best, for now."

"Yes …" Fletch said, uncertainly. "I guess so."

21

Before again pulling the drapes closed in his room at the Hotel Yellow Parrot, Fletch noticed that across the utility area the man was back painting the room. "If he doesn't finish soon," Fletch said to himself, "I'll go across and help him."

In bed again, hearing the samba drums from two or three combos in the street, Fletch tried his best to sleep. He breathed deeply, evenly, a long time, to convince his body he was asleep.

His body was not fooled. He was awake.

His mind was crowded with wriggling flesh, with people dressed as rabbits and rodents, harlequins and harlots, grandes dames and play school children, villains and viscounts, convicts and crooks, pirates and priests. *Clearly, you cannot sleep,* Laura had said. *Did you fall asleep?* Teo had asked. *I thought not.* With a fat Queen of Sheba eating cookies from a bag. With the sight of a man walking well with a long knife sticking out of his chest, reporting to police that he had lost his camera.

Idalina Barreto had been on the sidewalk in front of the Hotel Yellow Parrot when he returned. The wooden-legged great-grandson was with her. She had some sort of rag doll in her hand.

As he hurried into the hotel, she yelled and shook the rag doll at him.

Again he put the pillow over his head. Again he insisted he go to sleep. He thought how tired his legs were, from dancing with Jetta, from …

It was no good.

"*Bum, bum, paticum bum.*"

Heavily, he got out of bed. He opened the drapes again.

He looked up the number of Marilia Diniz in the telephone book.

"*Prugurundum.*"

He dialed her number. It rang five times.

"Marilia? Good morning. This is Fletcher."

"Good morning, Fletcher. Are you enjoying Carnival?"

"Marilia, I know it is Sunday morning, during Carnival; it is wrong of me to call; but I need to talk to you. I have not slept since Thursday."

"You must be enjoying Carnival."

"It is not exactly that. Are you too busy? Can we meet somewhere?"

"Right now?"

"If I don't get sleep soon … I don't know what will happen."

"Where's Laura?"

"She went to Bahia with her father. She'll be back later today."

"You need to see me, before you can sleep?"

"I think so. I need to understand something, do something. I need advice."

"You are disturbed?"

"I lack in understanding."

"Come over. Do you know how to get to Leblon?"

"Yes. I have your address from the telephone book. Are you sure it's all right if I come now?"

"I ignore Carnival. I am here."

"TROUBLE BETWEEN YOU AND LAURA?" Marilia asked.

In her little house in Leblon, behind a high wooden fence, Marilia Diniz led Fletch into a small study.

"I saw you in a car with the Tap Dancers yesterday."

Fletch did not dare ask her what time of day, or night, she saw them; whether all the Tap Dancers were blinking. "I relieved them of some money, playing poker."

At the side of the study, Marilia was adjusting a disk in a word processor. "The Brazilian male," she said, "is known for his energy."

"There's magic, high energy in the food."

"The Brazilian male is slow to give up his ... what? ... his immaturity." She started the word processor and watched it operate a moment. "At seventy, eighty, the Brazilian male is still a boy."

The word processor was whizzing away, typing manuscript. "Forgive me," Marilia said. "This is my routine for Sunday mornings, making manuscript of my week's work." She sat in a comfortable chair near her desk and indicated Fletch should sit on a two-person sofa. "I used to have a typist, but now? Another job lost. Teodomiro arranged this word processor for me."

Fletch sat.

"You look healthy enough," pale Marilia said. "Glowing."

"I have already been to the police station this morning. A woman I know, from California, showed up at my hotel yesterday morning, early. She had been robbed. I told her I would bring her money, immediately. Walking between my hotel and hers, she disappeared."

"Ah, Carnival ..."

"Really disappeared, Marilia. With Teo's help, I checked her suite at the Jangada. Her clothes are still there. She has no money, no passport, no credit cards, identification."

"You are right to be concerned," Marilia said. "Anything

can happen during Carnival. And does. Is there any way I can help you?"

"I don't think so. We went through the hospital for that district. Teo says I just must wait."

"Waiting is hard."

"That's not why I came to see you. As I said on the phone, I have not slept since Thursday."

"No one sleeps during Carnival." Then Marilia said, "So I guess you don't want any coffee."

"No, thanks. Do you know about this old woman who says I am her murdered husband come-back-to-life?"

"Someone mentioned something about it, the other night at Teo's." Marilia glanced at her word processor. "You tell me about it."

"Okay." On the divan, Fletch put his hands under his thighs. "When you, Laura, and I were having that drink at the café on Avenida Atlântica, Friday afternoon, an old woman in a long white dress came along the sidewalk and apparently saw me. She stopped near the curb. She stared at me until we left. Did you happen to notice her?"

"I'm ashamed to say I didn't."

"She was behind you."

"Is the old woman the reason you disappeared under the table?"

"No. That was because of this other woman, from California, who walked down the street just then. I was surprised to see her."

"The woman who has since disappeared?"

"Yes."

Marilia got up and checked her word processor, scanned the processed manuscript.

"When Laura and I entered the forecourt of the Yellow Parrot, this old hag jumped out of the bushes at us. She was screaming and pointing her finger at me. Laura talked to her calmly." Marilia sat down again and listened to Fletch expressionlessly. "The old woman said that she recognized me. In an earlier life, I had been her husband, Janio Barreto. That forty-seven years ago, at about my present age, I had been murdered. And now I must tell her who it was who had murdered me."

Marilia said nothing.

Fletch said, "Laura said, 'Clearly you will not rest until you do.'"

"And you have not rested."

"I have not slept."

"You think the old woman has put a curse on you?"

"Marilia, she hangs around outside my hotel, accosts me every time I go in or go out. She brought her great-grandchildren to the hotel to meet me. This morning she was there on the sidewalk, yelling at me and shaking some kind of a voodoo doll at me."

"A *calunga* doll."

"Whatever."

The word processor finished its work and turned itself off.

Marilia said, "An interesting story."

"No one will help me to understand," Fletch said. "Otavio Cavalcanti will answer none of my questions, about anything. He just nods and says, 'Yes.' Teo says he doesn't understand, doesn't know what to do. I can't understand whether Toninho Braga is making a joke out of it or whether there is some part of him that is serious. Worst of all, I can't understand Laura at all. She's an intelligent woman, a concert pianist. She seems to have no curiosity about my background, but she seems to give this Janio Barreto matter some credence."

Marilia sighed. "Ah, Brazil."

"I can't tell if everyone here is playing some kind of an elaborate joke, a trick on me."

"What do you think?"

"I don't know. Laura says I won't rest until I reveal this

murderer, and I haven't. Teo seems to say he is not surprised I am not sleeping. The Tap Dancers just don't expect me to sleep. How can I figure out what happened in Rio de Janeiro a generation before I was born? Am I to die of sleeplessness?"

"Did the old woman say you wouldn't sleep until you answered her?"

"I don't know. Laura talked to her. In Portuguese that was way above my head. I believe the old woman did say so. Why else would Laura have said so?"

"And you believe all this?"

"Of course not. But I'm nearly going crazy with sleeplessness."

Marilia's eyes traveled around the stacks of books in her study. "What's the question?"

"First, could this all be an immense practical joke Laura and the Tap Dancers are playing on me? The Tap Dancers seemed to know all about it before they ever met me."

"Could be," Marilia said.

"They're all friends. I'm the foreigner. Surely it is easy enough to hire an old woman, some children, a ten-year-old boy on a wooden leg?"

Marilia frowned. "A small boy on a wooden leg?"

"Yes. Supposedly the great-grandson. Named Janio Barreto, of course."

Marilia said, softly: "Or it could be that you are Janio Barreto, and you were murdered decades ago, and you have come back to Rio to reveal who murdered you."

Fletch stared at her. "Are you in on this, too?"

"Fletcher, my new friend from North America, you must understand that most of the people in this world believe in reincarnation, in one form or another." Marilia stood up and went to her word processor.

She began to tear and stack the pages of her manuscript.

"Marilia, may I point out to you that while you and I have been sitting in this room talking about ghosts and curses and *calunga* dolls, a magnificent, modern piece of technology quietly has been typing your manuscript in the corner?"

"This will not be read in your country." She placed the stack of new pages under a manuscript on her desk. "I am not translated and published in the United States of the North. The publishers, the people there have a different idea of reality, of what's important, what affects people, what happens, of life and death." She sat in her soft chair. "Have you at least had breakfast?"

"Yes."

"Then what shall we do?"

"Tell me straight out if I should take this matter seriously."

"It is serious, if you're not sleeping. You can become quite ill from not sleeping. You can drive your car into a lamp post."

"Marilia, nothing in my background prepares me for this. I was employed as an investigative reporter for a newspaper, dealing with real issues, police corruption—"

"This is not real?"

"Can it be real that I was murdered forty-seven years ago? That I have come back from the grave?"

Marilia chuckled. "It's real that you've come back to Rio de Janeiro. It's real that some old woman thinks so. It's real that you're not sleeping. Ah, Carnival!" Marilia said. "People go crazy during Carnival!"

"I don't intend to be one of them."

"Reconciling differing realities," Marilia apparently quoted from somewhere. "What does your education and training, as an investigative journalist, tell you to do in a situation which perplexes you?"

Fletch thought a short moment. "Find out the story."

"My training says that, too. So let's go find out the story. Where do the Barreto family live?"

"Someone mentioned … Toninho mentioned … Santos Lima. Toninho said I had lived in the favela Santos Lima."

"Let's go there, then." Marilia stood up and took a bunch of keys from her desk. "Let's go find out the story."

22

"Have you ever been in a favela before?" Marilia asked.

"I have been in slums before. In Los Angeles, New York, Chicago."

They had driven slowly past the Hotel Yellow Parrot. None of the Barreto family was at that time waiting in front of the hotel.

Fletch had parked the MP where Marilia told him to, on a city street a few blocks from the base of the favela.

"Last week, our industrial city of São Paulo produced ten thousand Volkswagen cars," Marilia said. "And twelve thousand, eight hundred and fifty babies. That is the reality of Brazil."

The favela of Santos Lima rose straight up a mountainside not all that far from the center of Rio de Janeiro. For the most part it was made of hovels stuck together by various materials, bits of lumber from here and there, packing crates, tar paper. A single roof might be made of over a hundred pieces of wood, tin, aluminum. A favorite patch was a flattened tin can nailed over a hole. A few were old, solid houses, all very small, and most of these had been painted at one time or another, purple, green, chartreuse. Some of the little stores, which mostly sold rice and beans and *chope*, looked somewhat permanent. As with most residential districts, the houses looked more solid, slightly more prosperous, the higher they were in the favela. The sewage from the higher houses flowed down muddy streets to settle under the lower houses.

As they entered the favela and began to climb, radios blared music from every direction. In a nearby shack, a packing crate really, a samba drum was being tuned. At a distance a large *bateria* of drums could be heard practicing.

Marilia Diniz and Fletch attracted much attention. Almost instantly they were surrounded by thirty, forty, fifty small children barefoot in the mud and sewage. The teeth of a few of the older children had rotted to stumps. Only a few of the very young had the distended bellies and skinny legs of malnutrition. Generally the bodies of the children old enough to fend and rummage for themselves, those over the age of six, although skinny, were well formed, as quick as darting fish. Their fingers tugged lightly at Marilia and Fletch; their imploring voices were low. For the most part, their eyes were bright.

"Well over half the population of Brazil is under nineteen years old," Marilia said. "And half of them are pregnant."

Marilia then asked the children for directions to the home of Idalina Barreto. In response, they fought for her hand to guide her there.

Fletch followed along with his own gaggle of children. Perhaps a dozen times he felt their hands slip into and out of the empty pockets of his shorts.

The women looked at him through their doorless doors and glassless windows with blank expressions on their worn faces, neither friendly nor unfriendly, not particularly curious. Their expressions indicated more that they were thinking about him, the life he led that they had glimpsed here and there; the big, clean buildings he had lived in, the airplanes he had flown in, the restaurants he had dined in, the accoutrements of his life, cars, telephones, air conditioners. There was little resentment in their look, as there was little resentment in their not being familiar with snow. His was a different life, vastly different, as different as if he had lived on Venus or Mars: too different to generate emotion.

A man called to Fletch in Portuguese from a bar counter under a tin roof. "Come! I'll buy you a little beer!"

"Thanks," Fletch answered in Portuguese. "Maybe later!"

And of course Fletch wondered about their lives as he walked through their world. To do without everything he knew, even a little money, privacy, machinery, in most cases, work. To do without everything but each other. He wondered if he could adapt to such a life, but only as he wondered if he could adapt to life on Jupiter or Saturn.

As they passed a small home, a toothless, bald old woman in a rocking chair in the shade looked at Fletch through rheumy eyes. "Janio!" she shrieked. "Janio Barreto!"

She tried to get out of her chair, but fell back.

Fletch just kept moving.

As they turned the corner around a sizable pink building, Fletch spotted young Janio Barreto down the dirt track. The boy hurried away on his wooden leg—doubtless, to broadcast the news that Fletch was coming.

The Barreto home was not very high in the favela.

Idalina Barreto stood tall in the door to her home, hands on her hips. Janio and other small children were in front of the house. Her eyes narrowed as Marilia and Fletch approached.

"*Bom dia*," Marilia said. She introduced herself. She explained that they had come to hear all about Janio Barreto and what had happened to him forty-seven years before.

The hag pointed to Fletch and, in her crackly voice, asked some question about Fletch.

Marilia said, "She wants to know if you will tell her what happened. Why you were murdered, and who murdered *you*."

There was no humor, no irony, in Marilia's face.

Sleepless, slightly dizzy in the bright sunlight, surrounded by a swarm of whispering children, Fletch shook his head. "I don't know."

As Idalina Barreto led Marilia and Fletch into her home, she dispatched children to find various relatives and bring them here.

The inside of the house was a space protected from some of the elements by walls of many boards of different shapes and sizes, nailed together at different angles under a patched tin roof.

The interior was impeccable. The dirt floor was reasonably dry and freshly swept. Plates, pans, cups, and glasses near the basin sparkled. A round table in the center of the room was polished. On it was a pretty embroidered cloth, and on the cloth was a bowl of fresh flowers. The *calunga* doll was also on the table. Chairs of various styles and sizes were around the walls of the room.

On the wall, either side of a battery radio, were magazine pictures of Jesus and the Pope.

A vast crowd was collecting outside the house.

Marilia said, "Idalina would like to know if you'd like coffee."

"Yes. Thank her."

Idalina flicked her wrist, and more children darted out.

Then she sat in a tall-backed wooden chair with wide arms. She gathered the hems of her long white dress around her ankles.

She indicated with a sweep of her hand that Marilia and Fletch should be seated in chairs of their choosing.

Fletch took a humble seat in a kitchen-styled chair.

As they waited silently, children brought them cups of very strong, very sweet coffee.

A few adults came into the room, four women, two men. They were introduced to Fletch as Idalina's children and grand-children. Fletch stood to greet each of them and didn't really get their names.

Each stared at him, round-eyed. They didn't seem willing or able to breathe normally. They backed into chairs along the walls.

Finally, the one for whom everyone apparently had been waiting arrived: a man in his fifties, shirtless, in proper black shorts and sandals. His hair was neatly combed.

"I speak English," he said, shaking Fletch's hand. "I am Janio Barreto Filho. I have worked many years as a waiter, in Copaca-bana." He stared into Fletch's eyes a long, breathless moment. Then, old enough to be Fletch's father, he said, "I am your son." In one movement, he hugged Fletch to him and embraced him hard. There was a choked sob in Fletch's ear. "We are so glad you have come back."

23

"I will speak English so good as I can," the middle-aged Janio Barreto Filho said. "Mother says to me you want me to bring to life for you the facts of what happened."

"Yes," Fletch said. "Please."

"If this will help you tell us who murdered you ..."

Barreto Filho sat in a cushioned chair along the back wall of the house. Stately as a duchess, Idalina Barreto sat in her tall chair along the side wall. Fletch and Marilia sat along the other side wall.

Adult relatives sat in the other chairs. Four stood near the door. Children sat on the dirt floor. The windows were filled with people listening.

The area in front of the house was crowded with people.

From somewhere in the neighborhood the distinct sound of a television ceased.

But, of course, practicing drums could still be heard.

As Janio Barreto Filho spoke, he was interrupted, questioned, reminded, and corrected by his mother and other adults inside and outside the house. Marilia helped to translate the difficult parts.

Listening intently, as the room under the tin roof in the sun became hotter, the air thicker, Fletch put together a continuous narrative to take away with him, to dissect and analyze later.

This may be a story, Janio Barreto Filho said, of a father who may have been right.

After all these years, my mother would like to know.

My father, Janio Barreto, was a handsome man, fair of hair and skin, well built, very lively, believed to be the best dancer in all the favela, maybe all of Rio de Janeiro. At least people say they enjoyed watching him the most. Sometimes, serving young people from North America, one or two from Chile or Argentina, in the hotels of Copacabana, I have thought of him, as this was always as he was described to me, light in color and as unconcerned with the sad little things in life as a rich person.

It is said he came from near São Paulo, perhaps the descendant of one of the North Americans from the South of the United States who came to that area at the end of your Civil War, to try to continue their plantation, slave-owning lives there. Many such came, and, of course, such is the beauty and seductiveness of our women, it was not long before they too became a part of the Brazilian population, their children having black and Indian blood and therefore unable to keep their brothers and sisters in bondage.

But you were truly fair, and came to the favela Santos Lima like a welcome thunderstorm in midwinter heat, casting your bolts of lightning everywhere. Why you came here, perhaps you could tell us now.

You were fourteen or fifteen when you arrived, full of your juices, full of laughs and smiles, being here, there, everywhere at once. As soon as you came to the favela, everyone could not have enough news of you: *Where is*

Janio? What has Janio done now? Did you hear what Janio did last night? When the pantaloons of the corrupt policeman were pasted on the statue of Saint Francis, when the new bicycle of the storekeeper was found in a bedroom of the brothel, when the shit-dam suddenly appeared around the big house a few of the faithful had built for the strict North American missionary, everyone knew you did it, and laughed with you, and stroked your fair hair.

The prestige of any girl you lay with rose in the favela. I suppose some of the girls lied about this, as it seems impossible to me—a man who enjoys life as much as any other—that one boy could have granted such prestige to so very many girls. In my own youth, being your acknowledged son, too much was expected of me. Going down the street I had to protect myself, not only from girls, but from their mothers as well. It is true that the favela Santos Lima is known to have many more fair people than any other favela in Rio de Janeiro.

Of course you took on friends, a gang of three or four boys, two of whom were Idalina's brothers. Together you spent the days on the beaches, wrestling, swimming, playing soccer, the nights drinking and dancing and gambling, increasing the prestige of girls individually and raising mischief.

Now, Idalina's father was a man of great dignity. Although he worked as a conductor on a trolley car, he spent his life studying to be a bookkeeper. He never succeeded in finding work as a bookkeeper, but he prepared himself. It was his fervent wish at least to hand on to his sons the idea of being a bookkeeper.

He did not share in the favela's general idolatry of Janio Barreto. He felt you were leading his sons astray, giving them a liveliness that was not natural to them or in keeping with the idea of keeping books.

Through people he knew at the samba school, finally he succeeded in getting his sons jobs on a fishing boat. But the old men who owned the fishing boat made the condition highly irksome to old Fernando that they would only hire his sons to work on the fishing boat if they could hire Janio Barreto as well. Whether the idea was that they believed my uncles needed your leadership and brains, even though at first you knew nothing about the sea, being from the interior of Brazil, or whether it was the idea of the elders to get you to sea and therefore away from the favela some hours of the week and therefore cut down on the mischief and population growth, or whether they wanted, by being your employers, to be the first to know and tell of your pranks is unknown to me. To get his sons employed, Fernando had no choice but to agree.

So you went on the fishing boat with the Gomes brothers, and soon there were stories of a dead cold fish five feet long being put in the bed of the most precise bachelor in the favela while he slept (it was sad he never slept in his bed or ate fish again), of a fishing-boat race which caused an older captain, whom you had taunted unmercifully, to become so determined to win at any cost that he rammed his own dock under full sail at such high speed he smashed his boat to slivers.

Fernando put up with all this with resignation. At least his sons had jobs, and there was hope that after a while working hard at sea, they would come to the idea of bookkeeping.

But when you began to call upon his daughter Idalina, coo to her through the window, spread flowers you stole from the cemetery all over the roof of the house, Fernando went into a rage.

Nor did he consider it funny when, on the night of his Saint's Day and perhaps he had had a bit too much to drink and lay in a stupor, you came along and shaved off only half of his mustache.

Then, at the age of eighteen, when most young men consider it wise and appropriate to be humble, apparently goaded by Fernando's open disapproval of you, you announced to the whole favela your intention of making Idalina your wife.

The favela was delighted. They knew marriage would do you no harm, not slow you down or make you less entertaining.

Idalina was delighted. It did not disturb her to be marrying the liveliest boy in the favela, or that her bond to you in marriage would have to be made of elastic.

Fernando fell into a mood so black for weeks he could not think of bookkeeping. He spent his time keeping his eye on Idalina. He argued with the air.

"Am I the only sane man in the world to see that Janio Barreto is a bad boy and no match for my Idalina? He has done enough to me, in keeping my sons from thinking in assets and debits! Why does he want a wife when he has every girl in the favela spitting at each other over him? He will never stop! Does he want to marry my daughter and continue his wild life just to torment me? It is as natural for him to be a husband as it is for a tomcat to pull a wagon!

"Idalina, he is no good! At the first difficulties of life, he will wander away! Already he has wandered from his home once! I want to know why! Once a man has wandered from his home, he is never to be trusted! He will wander again!

"Believe me, he will end up beaten in a gutter! That will not be a husband to be proud of!

"Probably dead! Some day someone will put a knife to him, and that will be the end of your husband, Janio Barreto, and of your marriage!"

The weight of the favela was on the side of the young lovers, of course, as people who are not directly involved in a situation always prefer romance to reason, and while Fernando stewed in his deep gloom, you and Idalina were married.

Now, as you must remember, not only were you known to be able to dance better and for a longer time than anyone, with more admiring eyes upon you, also you brought to the favela many new things about kick-dancing, capoeira, it being a skill which really developed in the interior. You taught the young men in Santos Lima more about capoeira than people knew in all the other favelas in Rio.

At that time, the Carnival Parade was beginning to become more organized from just a street competition among the favelas to the more formal presentation and attraction it is today.

Immediately, the samba school of Santos Lima became most famous for its troupe of capoeiristas you had trained. Santos Lima still has the reputation as having the best capoeira group in Rio de Janeiro.

But the first prophecy of Fernando came true.

You did not return immediately from Carnival that year. For days afterwards you were missing.

Finally you returned to Santos Lima from somewhere

in the city. It was clear you had been physically beaten, and very badly. Your body was black with bruises. There were knife cuts on your upper arms and shoulders. Your face was as lumpy and welted as the bed of a couple married fifty years. You dragged yourself home like a beaten dog. Obviously, you had ended up beaten in a gutter.

People remarked, in hushed voices, the change in you. Silently you sat in your little house, licking your wounds. You never said what happened. You spoke to no one. Your laughter was not heard anywhere in the favela. You never went out and embarrassed Idalina by being with other women, to such an extent Idalina was beginning to lose her pride in you.

This is as I have the story from my mother and my uncles. Is your life beginning to come alive for you?

Then the second prophecy of Fernando came true.

After sitting quietly at home, not working, not playing, for almost all of Lent, you rose up and, carrying nothing, taking nothing with you except the working shorts you wore roped around your waist, you walked down the favela without a salutation to anyone, and disappeared. You wandered away.

Everyone was sure you were gone for good. Fun had gone from the favela.

Everyone commiserated with Fernando for having an abandoned daughter and two small grandchildren living out of his pocket, and congratulated him on the accuracy of his prophecies.

But the next winter, nine months later, you came back. You sailed into Guanabara Bay in a fishing boat you said was your own, a big boat ten meters long. You said you won it playing cards in Uruguay. The name painted on her side was in Spanish, *La Muñeca*. Surely you had sailed a long way. You were as thin as a street dog and very badly sunburned across your nose and shoulders. Some people said you went to Uruguay and stole the boat. Did you?

So now you had your own fishing boat.

In the inactivity caused by your absence, one of the Gomes brothers had become too fat to fish, the other too drunken. They both said they wanted to stay ashore now and think about bookkeeping.

You took on another young man, younger than you, named Tobias Novaes, to help you fish.

You worked hard. Shortly, you had a house near the top of the favela, higher even than Fernando's house. And for every married year, you had a child from your wife, Idalina. And every one of those children had children to play with their own ages who were also partly fair and looked as much like them as cousins.

At about your present age, it happened that a girl younger than you, who was as fair of hair and skin as yourself, came to the favela. Immediately, the favela said, "Oh, poor Idalina! This one will be serious! If they love themselves, how can they not love each other?"

And it was noticed that you became more serious then, worked longer hours, seldom looked up from your work. It was if you were trying to ignore the inevitable: Ana Tavares, her name was.

But the inevitable is the inevitable, and as if your seed were transmitted by the wind, it was soon seen that Ana Tavares was glowing in her pregnancy.

This was especially noted as Ana Tavares was only waiting out the year to be old enough to join the convent of the Sacred Heart of Jesus. People marveled that a girl who spent so many hours of the day and the night kneeling before the statue of the Blessed Virgin could become pregnant. They attributed it to the wind.

Spending just as much time in prayer as always, Ana did not explain or complain.

Her father, however, whose life had not been as saintly as is recommended, was outraged. It had been his fondest wish to have a daughter a nun to pray for his soul before and after it departed.

You, having no father or brothers to attack, and being too young and strong, too expert a capoeirista, to attack, laughed for days after old Tavares attacked your father-in-law, Fernando, for his troublemaking son-in-law. Your father-in-law did not defend you. He too carried such rage at you that he yelled back at Tavares, and the two fathers of women became so enraged thinking about you that soon they were beating each other with their fists, then rolling on the ground, apparently fighting about which had the greater rage against you.

In truth, the son of Ana Tavares was entirely fair. She became the wife of a carpenter, and the boy—most likely another of your sons—became a *Puxador de Samba*, a singer of great repute in the samba school.

Yes, Oswaldinho there, in the window, is a son of that son of yours. You see how fair he is? Clearly, he has your blood, as have I.

Then the third prophecy of old Fernando came true—really came true.

One night you did not come home. You did not come home most nights. You were still young and perhaps by now considered it your obligation to entertain the favela with your tricks and to continue increasing your ever-growing audience by copulation.

But after this night in particular, after a heavy sea storm, you were found on the beach, face down, with your throat slit ear to ear. Your blood had drained from your neck into the sand. Your shorts and hair and skin were caked with salt water, as if you had swum a long way to shore.

People say that in that particular spot on the beach, it has been impossible to light a fire or even light a match, ever since.

Your boat, *La Muñeca*, was missing, and never seen again.

Never seen again also was the boy who had helped you on the boat, Tobias Novaes.

For many years it was believed you had been murdered by young Tobias, although that surprised people, as it was generally believed he was a good boy. People thought he had slit your throat and stolen your boat.

But years later, his father got a letter from him, saying he had become a monk in Recife. Instantly, they had a letter written to him, asking if he had murdered you and stolen your boat.

The answer came back, eventually, that he hadn't known you were dead and that he felt himself greatly indebted to you as it was your example, and the example of your life, which had made the unworldly, serene, contemplative life of a monk seem so ideal to him.

For all these years your murder has been a mystery. There were so many people who could have killed you. Someone in the favela who did not like a trick you played on him? Did Tobias murder you for the boat? Did Uruguayans come and murder you and take back their boat? Or had the boat wrecked in the storm? How about old Tavares? He believed your preventing his daughter, Ana, from becoming a nun, surely condemned him to hell …?

My grandfather Fernando made three predictions about you. That you would end up beaten in the gutter. You were beaten up, but you survived it, became your old self again. That, sooner or later, you would wander away. You did, but you came back. That some day, someone would take a knife to you and kill you. That happened.

My mother, Idalina, who is very old now, as you see, wants to know the truth of these things. Who murdered you, and why?

How is it that her father was so right about you?

24

"What Laura says is true," Fletch said to Marilia Diniz across the lunch table. "Anyone can tell you any story, and say it is the past."

Leaving favela Santos Lima totally unsatisfied, Fletch and Marilia led a parade of plucking pixies and curious adults down the hill and along the city street to his car. He had made his courtesies, thanked Janio Barreto Filho for the story, shaken hands with all the adults, thanked Idalina for her coffee and hospitality, generally wished the favela well in the parade of the samba schools that night, but left the airless little house as soon as he could. The heat in the room had become almost unbearable. But the eyes of everyone told him how unsatisfied they were. They had expected the story of Janio Barreto to bring his memories alive so he could tell them before leaving who had been his murderer.

Solemnly, Fletch promised he would think over the whole story.

He and Marilia drove to Colombo, a sparkling clean tearoom noted for its great pastry.

Marilia asked, "Do you still think it is a joke being played on you by Laura and the Tap Dancers?"

"I don't see how it can be. All those people in the door and windows, all those people in the street had heard the story before, knew parts of it well enough to correct Janio, add elements to it— and all with high seriousness. If it is a trick, it's the most elaborate trick conceivable."

Their waffles were warm and tender.

"You have heard the story now," Marilia said. "What is the answer?"

"How would I know?"

Marilia's eyes flickered at him. "All right. But use what you do know, use your training. You were trained as an investigative reporter ..."

"Yeah: investigating how come the city's water pipes run an extra five kilometers to avoid the property owned by the water commissioner. Big deal. This is not quite the same sort of situation."

"Nevertheless ..."

"Investigative reporters do not make guesses just to satisfy people with a conclusion to a story."

"But investigative reporters do think, don't they?"

"Think about documented facts. How can I think about something that happened on a beach in Rio de Janeiro forty-seven years ago? However long I am in Brazil, I will never be that prescient. Or postscient."

"What will you tell them?"

Fletch made sure there was syrup on each part of his waffle. "I suppose I'll tell them the kindest thing I can think of: Uruguayans came and slit his throat and took their boat back. It would be kinder than blaming someone in the favela dead or alive."

"Janio said he won the boat playing cards." Marilia chewed thoughtfully. "There is some evidence he did."

"What evidence?"

"If you stole a boat, even from a different country, wouldn't you change its name?"

"Of course. I suppose so."

"The name of the boat was in Spanish. *La Muñeca.* He never changed its name. They said after Janio was found dead, *La Muñeca* was missing. Never seen again."

Fletch sighed.

Marilia said, "And if Uruguayans killed Janio Barreto, why didn't they kill Tobias Novaes as well? He would have been on the boat with Janio."

"Perhaps the Uruguayans appeared after they docked."

"Could be," Marilia said.

"After Tobias wandered off to become a monk. Marilia, that's too big a coincidence in timing. How could Tobias wander off to become a monk without telling anyone what he was doing, just before Janio got his throat slit?"

"There had been a storm at sea. I have heard of people becoming very religious, very suddenly, during storms at sea. They make deals. *Spare my life, oh Lord, and I will devote the rest of my life to singing Thy praises.*"

"Maybe."

"I think the boat sank. And both Janio and Tobias swam ashore. Tobias to join a monastery; Janio to get his throat slit."

"That's fine. It's great to guess. But how can we know?"

Again, Marilia's eyes flickered.

Fletch said, "Tobias himself is a good bet as the murderer. Surely he wouldn't be the first to commit a heinous crime and then, after a while, so weighted with guilt, he hies off to a monastery to spend the rest of his life atoning."

"True. Tobias could have killed Janio. He could have stolen the boat. But after years of being a monk, could he have lied about it?"

Somewhat in imitation of Tito Granja, Fletch crossed his eyes.

"After years of atonement," Marilia said, "Tobias would know he would be risking his soul to lie."

"'Risking his soul.'" Fletch repeated. "That brings up the father of the girl who was going to be a nun. What was his name? Tavares. Apparently he thought he was going to end up in hell anyway. Why wouldn't he have killed Janio?"

"He might have. Still, murder is the greatest crime. And there is always the possibility of personal salvation."

Fletch looked at Marilia's bracelet. It was made of rotting braided cloth. He had seen many such bracelets in Brazil. He had difficulty understanding the significance of them.

"Fernando," Fletch said. "Idalina's father. Certainly he hated Janio. Over a long period of time. He got into a fistfight over him."

"Kill his son-in-law? Leave his daughter a widow, his grand-children fatherless?" Slowly, Marilia said, "I suppose so. Fernando apparently thought Janio not a very good husband or father."

"And he had reason to be envious of him. Fernando could never find work as a bookkeeper. Then Janio shows up with his own boat. Becomes a prosperous man. Even gets to live in a house higher up in the favela than Fernando."

Marilia, a slim, trim woman, surprised Fletch by ordering one of the bigger, more sugary pastries.

Fletch said, "You know, once you make prophecies about someone, there is the instinct to help them become fulfilled."

"Fernando said someone would take a knife to Janio and kill him, and it wasn't happening fast enough to satisfy Fernando, so he did the job himself?"

"I suppose prophets have to work at their reputations, as much as anyone else."

"Mmmmm. So what will you do, Fletcher? What will you tell these people?"

"I don't know. I'm not about to point the finger at a monk. Or at the grandfather of the family. Or at the memory of some other deceased citizen whose daughter was deflowered by the victim. Any one of hundreds of people could have done in Janio."

"Now that you've heard the story, will you be able to sleep?"

"Will I?"

They finished their pastries in silence.

Fletch said, "Marilia, tell me about that bracelet you're wearing."

Self-consciously she touched it with the fingers of her other hand. "Oh, that."

"I see many people, men and women, wearing these cloth, braided bracelets."

"Just a superstition, I guess." Her face flushed. "You make a wish, you know, for something you hope will come true. As you make the wish, you put on this braided bracelet. You wear it until what you wished for comes true."

"Supposing what you wish for doesn't come true?"

Slightly red-faced, she laughed. "Then you wear in until it falls off."

"You believe in such a thing?"

"No," she said quickly.

"But you're wearing such a bracelet."

"Why not?" she asked, resetting it on her wrist. "It does no harm to act as if you believe in such a thing, just in case it is true."

OUTSIDE THE RESTAURANT they stopped at a kiosk. Marilia bought *Jornal do Brasil* and Fletch bought *Brazil Herald* and the *Latin America Daily Post*.

A healthy-seeming, curly-haired man of about thirty was leaning against Fletch's MP. It appeared he was waiting for them.

He spoke rapidly, happily to Fletch.

Then, seeing he wasn't being understood, he spoke to Marilia.

She answered him, happily enough. While talking with him, she opened the small purse tied to her wrist, took out some money, and gave it to him.

The man stuffed the money into his shoe.

Then he leaned against the next car, a Volkswagen bug.

In the car, Fletch asked, "What did he want?"

"Ohhhh. He said he had been taking care of the car for us while we were away. It is for him to take care of the cars along this section of curb, he said."

"Is it?"

"He says so."

"Who gave him charge of this section of curb?"

"No one. It is just something he says."

Fletch started the car. "If it is just something he says, then why did you give him money? Why didn't you just tell him to get lost?"

Flustered, Marilia was looking into her handbag, perhaps rearranging the interior. "I suppose I owe it to him because I just had such a nice lunch."

25

"Fletch?"

"Yes?"

"Toninho Braga, Fletch. Look what time it is."

"Shortly after noon."

"That's right. And so far no one has reported finding Norival's body."

Over the phone, Toninho's voice sounded more hushed than alarmed.

Fletch had driven Marilia Diniz to her home in Leblon, thanked her for accompanying him to the favela, repeated he still had no way of solving a forty-seven-year-old murder mystery, but he would return to the hotel to try to sleep.

His room at the Hotel Yellow Parrot had been cleaned. The unslept-in bed had been freshly made up.

He telephoned the Hotel Jangada and asked for Joan Collins Stanwyk in Room 912.

No answer.

Across the utility area, the man was still painting the room.

He was about to strip, to shower, to darken the room, to

get into bed again, to try to sleep, when the phone rang.

"Toninho," he said. "It's Sunday. A big day of Carnival. Communication is slow."

"That's exactly it, Fletch. There would have been hundreds, thousands of people on that beach, shortly after dawn."

"Finding a body—"

"Norival is not just a body. He is a Passarinho. That would be news."

"First the police have to be summoned—"

"Yes, the police would be summoned. But we left plenty of identification on Norival's body. The people who found the body would be quick to tell the Passarinho family, the radio stations. The police would be even quicker. They would compete for the attention of the Passarinho family."

"I don't see what you're saying. You put Norival's body in the water. He was dead. He has to come ashore somewhere, sometime, if you were right about the tides."

"I was right about the tides. Where's Norival?"

"How would I know?"

Fletch looked down at the soft, smooth countenance of the bed.

"Fletch, we must go make sure someone finds the body of Norival."

"Toninho, I'm not sure I can take many more disappearances today, of persons dead and alive."

"You must come help us look, Fletch. That will make four of us. We can comb the beach."

"You want to go beachcombing for a corpse?"

"What else can we do? We put Norival's body there to be found, not to be lost. What if he were lost forever? There would be no funeral mass. He would not be properly buried. His family might think he ran away."

"His boat would be missing."

"Sailed away. To Argentina! Think of his poor mother!"

"His poor mother."

"Such a thing would kill her. Not to know what happened to her son."

"Toninho … I still have not slept."

"That's all right."

"'All right'?"

"You must help us. Four searching is better than three searching. It is a long beach."

"Toninho …"

"We'll pick you up in ten minutes."

The phone line died.

26

"Perhaps we should check with Eva," Tito said. "Norival might have gone back to her."

"Norival was happy with Eva," Orlando said.

Of the four young men walking along the beach, only Fletch wore sandals. He knew himself not sufficiently carioca to walk along a beach in the midday sun in bare feet.

Toninho, Tito, and Orlando had picked Fletch up in the black four-door Galaxie.

On the sidewalk in front of the hotel, the youngest Janio Barreto on a wooden leg silently watched Fletch get into the car and be driven away.

The drive to the beach where Orlando was scheduled to appear had been as fast as possible through the Carnival crowds.

At one place on Avenida Atlântica perhaps as many as a thousand people in tattery costumes jumped up and down around a big samba band moving forward only a few meters an hour on the back of a flatbed truck. Never had he seen so much human energy spent in so little forward motion.

On the way to the beach they listened silently to the loud car radio.

The discovery of Norival Passarinho's body was not yet news.

The beach was filled with bright umbrellas, mats. Families and other groups picnicked and played.

Orlando said to Fletch: "It is said if a person dies copulating, he is guaranteed to return to life soon."

"For Norival, the process might have been very quick," said Tito.

Spread apart only somewhat, they walked along the water's edge, looking for Norival perhaps washed up dead but thought asleep, some crowd of gossips with news of something unusual having happened, the corpse of the Passarinho boy being found, police barriers, markers, something, anything.

"Do people say the same thing in the United States of North America?" Orlando asked.

"I don't think so," Fletch said. "I never heard it."

"People in the United States of North America don't die while copulating," Toninho said. "They die while talking about it."

"They die while talking to their psychiatrists about it," Orlando laughed.

"Yes, yes," said Toninho. "They die worrying about copulating."

"People of the United States of North America," Tito scoffed. "This is how they walk."

Tito began to move hurriedly over the sand, his head and shoulders forward of his body, legs straight, not pivoting his hips at all, his hands dangling loosely beside him like a couple of cow udders, his eyes staring straight ahead, an expectant grin on his face, each foot landing flat on the sand. The impression was of a body being pushed at the shoulders, falling forward, each foot coming out and landing at the last second to keep the body from falling flat on its face.

Fletch stopped walking and laughed.

For a while, then, he walked slightly behind his friends.

"Yes," Tito said. "Norival may have revived."

Fletch asked, "Is it true everyone goes slightly crazy during Carnival?"

Toninho said, "Slightly."

"If the way to life eternal," Fletch asked, "is to die copulating, then why don't people just copulate constantly?"

Orlando sniffed. "I do my best."

A man carrying two metal cylinders containing iced maté passed them. Each container easily weighed one hundred pounds. He would sell the maté in little cups to people on the beach. The man was in his sixties and he was walking rapidly enough to pass the four young men. His legs looked like the roots of trees hardened by time.

"This is crazy," Fletch said. Perhaps lying in the sun on the beach would make him drowsy enough to sleep.

Dead wallets, stolen and emptied, were on the beach like birds shot from the sky.

Toninho scanned the surface of the ocean. "There is not even a sign of his boat. That, too, should have come ashore."

"The boat sank," Tito said.

"Maybe Norival sank," Orlando said.

"Maybe Norival is alive and we are dead," Fletch said.

Orlando looked at him as if he had just offered a possibility worth consideration.

They were coming to the end of the beach.

Nearby was a group of very young teenage girls in bikinis. Five of the eight were pregnant.

Toninho said, "Absolutely, Norival was to come ashore somewhere along here."

"Let's ask," Fletch said. "Let's ask the people on the beach if they've noticed a Passarinho floating by without a boat."

"It leaves only one thing to do," Toninho said.

"Go home to bed," Fletch said.

"Swim along the beach," Toninho said.

"Oh, no," Fletch said.

Toninho was looking into the water. "It is possible Norival is lurking somewhere just below the surface."

"That would be just like Norival," Orlando said. "Playing some trick."

"*Arigó*," Toninho said.

"I need sleep," Fletch said. "Not a swim."

"Yes," Tito said, "Norival was apt to be a bit slow, sometimes, to show up."

"Last night, when I swam into Norival," Toninho said, "he was more under the surface than I would have expected."

"Right," said Tito. "We shall swim along the shore and see if we bump into Norival."

"Oh, no," said Fletch.

"Leave your sandals here," said Orlando. "Not even a North American can swim well wearing sandals."

ON THE WAY BACK in the car they listened to a long news broadcast. Mostly, it was about Carnival Parade that night, and certain controversies which had arisen concerning it. One samba school was insisting the theme they had chosen to present had been usurped a little bit by another samba school. At least, the themes of the two schools were believed by one school to be dangerously similar.

In all that long broadcast, the discovery of the corpse of Norival Passarinho was not reported.

27

"You're not becoming a Brazilian," Laura Soares said over the dinner table. "You're becoming a Carnival Brazilian."

When Fletch dragged himself back to his room at the Hotel Yellow Parrot, sunburned, caked with salt, the bottoms of his feet fried from just the walk up the beach from the ocean to the car, Laura was waiting for him, curled up in a chair studying sheet music, full of questions about where they would dine, full of enthusiasm for spending the night watching the Carnival Parade from Teodomiro da Costa's box.

Tiredly, he greeted her. She helped him shower. On the bed he wanted to sleep. She teased him into giving her a warmer greeting than he thought possible in his sleepless condition. They showered again.

She was dressing when he came out of the bathroom.

On the white trousers and white shirt he had laid out to wear that night, she had placed a wide, bright red sash.

"Is this for me?" he asked.

"From Bahia."

"Am I to wear it?"

"To the Carnival Parade. You will look very Brazilian."

"I am to wear a red sash without a coat?"

"Why would anyone wear a coat over such a beautiful red sash?"

"Wow." After he dressed, she helped him adjust it. "I feel like a Christmas present."

"You are a Christmas present. A jolly Christmas present wrapped in a red ribbon for Laura."

They decided to dine in the dining room which was on the second floor of the Hotel Yellow Parrot.

Through the floor-to-ceiling open windows they could see the *macumba* fires on Praia de Copacabana. Believers spend the night on the beach tending a fire, having written a wish, or the name of their illness, on a piece of paper which they launch in the first moments of the outgoing tide. On the first night of the year especially there are thousands of fires on the beach.

The hotel restaurant was said to be one of the best in the world. It was rare in that the restaurant's kitchen was exactly twice as big as the seating area.

They ordered *moqueca*, another Bahian specialty.

"You did not even read Amado's *Dona Flor and Her Two Husbands* while I was gone."

"Tell me about it."

"You said you could not sleep, of course, but you did not even read."

"Somehow I kept busy."

"Gambling with the Tap Dancers?"

"I relieved them of some of their inheritances."

"I dare not even ask you about this country inn they took you to."

"It had a swimming pool."

"Riding around all day. So late to the Canecão Ball. Cristina said you were dressed as a movie cowboy."

"An outfit I borrowed from Toninho."

"I saw it in the closet."

"I looked real sleek."

"That you danced hours with that French film star, Jetta."

"There was no one else to dance with her."

"I'm sure." Laura mixed her *pirão* with her *farofa com dendê*. "Brazilians are not like this all the time. Only during Carnival. Brazilians are a very serious people."

"I'm sure."

"Look at our big buildings. Our factories. Our biggest-in-the-world hydroelectric plant. Everything here runs by computer now. At the airport, all the public announcements, in each language, are done by computer voices. And you can understand what they are saying perfectly."

Through the window Fletch started to count the *macumba* fires on the beach.

"Marilia Diniz and I went this morning to the favela Santos Lima to see the Barreto family, to hear the story of Janio Barreto's life and death."

Laura did not seem interested in that. "You should read the novels of Nélida Piñon. Then you would know something of Brazilian life. Not just Carnival foolishness. Things are very different here in Brazil."

"I know," he said. "The water goes down the drain counterclockwise."

"Anyway …" She removed a bone from her fish. "Last night, in Bahia, I agreed finally to do this concert tour."

"Concert tour? You're going on a concert tour?"

"Pianists who stop playing the piano stop being pianists," she said.

"Where are you going? When?"

"In about a month. Bahia first, then São Paulo, Rio de

Janeiro, Recife. Friends of my father have been urging me to do this, setting it up for some time."

"I guess they want you to get serious."

"I am an educated pianist. I've had good reviews. I like the idea of bringing so much Brazilian music to the piano."

"You will have to work very hard to go on such a tour."

"Very hard."

"Practice a lot."

"A very lot."

"Do you want dessert?"

"Of course."

They ordered cherry tarts.

"Fletcher," she asked, "what are you serious about?"

"Sleeping."

"Serious."

"I'm serious about sleeping."

"Sleeping is necessary, I guess."

"I am seriously worried. You remember that woman I was to have breakfast with yesterday morning at the Hotel Jangada?"

"Who is she?"

"The woman in the green dress we saw on the avenida."

"You didn't want to see her."

"I do now. Her name is Joan Collins Stanwyk. She's from California."

"That was clear, from looking at her. Her eyes looked as if she were watching a movie."

"She's disappeared."

"People disappear in Brazil, Fletch." Laura didn't seem to want to hear about that, either. "What time are we to arrive at Carnival Parade?"

"Teo suggested about ten o'clock. I doubt he'll be there much earlier than that."

"I've never watched Carnival Parade from a box before."

"I think he suspects this is the only year I'll be here for it."

Laura said nothing.

For a moment, Fletch watched her finish her cherry tart.

Then Fletch gazed through the window at the *macumba* fires on the moonless beach. A cheer was sent up from a samba crowd on the avenida.

He said, "Carnival ..."

"The point of it is to remember that things are not always as they appear."

28

"Welcome to the Samba School Parade!" Teodomiro da Costa said in the tone of a ringmaster. He stood just inside the door of his box overlooking the parade route. He wore jeans and a T-shirt. On front of the T-shirt were printed a black bow tie and ruffles. In a more personal tone, he asked, "Have you eaten?"

"At the hotel."

He looked into Fletch's eyes and spoke just loudly enough for Fletch to hear him over the fantastic noise. "You have not slept."

"Not yet."

"Have a drink."

"Guarana, please."

Teo repeated the order to the barman.

"Laura!" Teo hugged her to his chest. "Did Otavio get home all right?"

"Of course. He just pretended to need help."

"I think that's what you do with daughters. You pretend to need their help when, actually, you do."

The box was bigger than Fletch had expected, big enough for

twenty people to move around in comfortably, to see, even dance, plus room for the sandwiches and drinks table, the barman.

Adrian Fawcett, the writer for the *Times*, was there, the Vianas, the da Silvas, the London broker and his wife, the Italian racing car driver and his girlfriend. Jetta looked at Fletch with the resentment of someone who had been danced with but not loved. She did not look at Laura at all.

Everyone marveled at everyone else's costumes, of course. Laura was dressed as an eighteenth-century musician, in breeches and knee socks, ruffled shirt front, gray wig. The Viana woman asked Laura if she had brought her piano to accompany her costume.

As Fletch moved forward in the box, glass of guarana in hand, he had the sensation that Rio's volume knob was being turned up. Thousands of drums were being played in the area. Hundreds of thousands of people were singing and chattering and cheering.

Across the parade route, the stands were a sea of faces inclined toward the sky. Above the bright lights aimed on the route, thick, hot, smoky air visibly rolled up the stands and formed a thin gray cloud overhead.

"Rio de Janeiro's Carnival Parade Class One-A is the biggest, most amazing human spectacle in the world," Teodomiro da Costa had said, inviting Fletch. "Except war."

The parade starts at six o'clock Sunday afternoon and continues until past noon Monday. About twelve samba schools, of more than three thousand costumed people each, compete in the parade.

"I'm not sure I can stand three more days of Carnival." Even speaking over the noise, Adrian Fawcett's voice was a deep rumbling chuckle. "Days of elation or depression have the same effect on people, you know. I'm drained already."

"It's a mark of character to be able to survive Carnival intact," Laura answered. "It's a matter of having the right attitudes."

She beamed at Fletch.

Fletch said: "It's all beyond belief."

"Next is Escola Guarnieri." Teo peered over the rail at the *bateria* in the bull pen. "Yes, that's Guarnieri." Then he said to Fletch, "After that comes Escola Santos Lima."

The parade route, on Avenida Marquês de Sapucaí, is only a mile long.

To the left along the parade route are the stands, built as high as most buildings, crammed with tens of thousands of people. They arrive in the stands, take and protect their seats, bake in the sun, eat their sandwiches, hold their bladders, chatter and sing beginning at noon, a full six hours before the parade starts. Almost all stay in their seats for the full twenty-four hours.

To the right along the parade route are the boxes, vastly expensive vantage points, some done up in bunting. In the boxes are government dignitaries, Brazilian and foreign celebrities, and people who are simply rich.

The parade route between its two sides is as wide as a three-lane road.

It is as wide as the line between shade and sun, sickness and health, tin and gold.

Also along the right-hand side of the route, ten meters high in the air, are the watchtowers where sit the various parade judges, one for costumes, one for floats, one for music, one for dancing, etc. They sit immobile, expressionless, alone, many behind dark sunglasses so that not even a flicker of an eye may be a subject of comment and controversy. Their names are not released to the public until the day of the parade. And so complicated and controversial is their task that the results of their judging are not announced until four days later, on Thursday.

Diagonally across the parade route from da Costa's box, to the left, is the bull pen filled with hundreds of costumed *ritmistas*, the *bateria* of drummers of Escola Guarnieri. Their drums are of all sizes and tones. It takes the drummers up to an hour to put themselves into their proper places in regard to each other, to get their rhythms up, their sound up. Now their rhythm and their sound are full, and fill everyone at the parade, fill their ears, their brains, their entire nervous systems, control the beatings of their hearts, make their eyes flush with blood, their hands and feet move involuntarily, their bones to vibrate. This is total sound, amplified only by human will, as primitive a sound as man ever made, the sound of drums, calling from every human, direct, immediate response, equalizing them in their numbness before the sound.

Everyone in da Costa's box is standing at the rail. Laura has taken off her wig and opened the collar of her eighteenth-century-styled shirt. The faces of everyone at the rail shine with sweat. Their eyes, their lips protrude slightly, as if the sound of the drums reverberating within them were seeking a way to burst out of them. The veins at their temples throb visibly to the beat of the drums. Being host, Teo stands back behind the people at the rail. Being tall, he can still see everything.

Down the parade route from the left, passing the *bateria* in the bull pen like the top of a T comes the *Abre-Alas*, the opening wing of Guarnieri's presentation. This group of *sambistas*, moving of course to the sound of the drums, wear bright, ornate, slightly exaggerated costumes presenting a hint of the time and place of the samba school's theme, in this case nineteenth-century Amazon plantation ball gowns, their hoop skirts a little too wide, the bodices a little too grand, the bouffants a little too high; for the men, spats a little too long, frock coats a little too wide in the shoulders, top hats a little too high. This is the slave's view of plantation life. The exaggeration is a making fun. The exaggeration also expresses victory over such a life.

Immediately behind the *Abre-Alas* comes a huge float stating the literary theme of Guarnieri's presentation. On the slowly moving truck invisible beneath the float is a mammoth book open for all to see the letters G. R. E. S. GUARNIERI (Gremio Recreativo Escola de Samba Guarnieri). It is desired that the spectator know that it is of history that the school portrays, a kind of written, authoritative history, which may be a kind of joke, too, or an exaggeration, as there is very little authoritative, written history.

Then comes the *Comissão de Frente*, a line of formally dressed men doing a strolling samba. It is desired that the spectators accept these aging *sambistas*, honored for their contributions to past Carnival Parades, chosen for their grace and dignity, as the samba school's board of directors. Few, if any, actually are directors. The real directors are working hard in the school's parade, all sides of it at once. The presentation dancers, drummers, floats on trucks and flatbeds, floats that are pushed by hand—must move at exactly one mile an hour, without gaps or holes, keeping the balances of colors and movements perfect.

Behind this line of dignitaries comes the first and most distinguished dancing couple, the *Porta Bandeira* and the *Mestre Sala*, the Flag Bearer and the Room, or Dancing Master. These are mature people, in their prime, dressed in lavish eighteenth-century costumes regardless of the theme, those decided by everyone in the favela to be absolutely the best dancers, those dancers everyone else most enjoys watching. Their dance step is incredibly complicated, to most people an incomprehensible wonder, with patterns within patterns, movements within movements. They too must move forward in their dancing at exactly one mile per hour. And while she dances, the lady of the couple must carry a flag, the samba school's emblem on one side, the symbol of that year's theme on the other side, waving it so that both sides are visible to everyone.

It is obligatory that every person in the parade, every dancer, dignitary, drummer, director working or parading must constantly be singing the *samba enredo*, the song presented by that school that year, as loudly and as well, as continuously, as he or she can.

As the *Alas* come by, the theme of the school's presentation becomes more and more clear, however broad the theme may be. An *ala* is a group of hundreds of vigorously dancing people identically dressed depicting some aspect of the theme. Here one *ala* is costumed as Indians from the Amazon basin, dancing steps suggestive of that cultural area. Another *ala* is again of plantation life, the costumes modified, of course, so that the beauty of the people of that favela, their flesh and movement, the joy of the dancers' bodies may be revealed and enjoyed by all.

In among the *alas* come the *Figuras de Destaque*, the prominent figures which relate to the theme, in this case mythically huge figures of Amazonian plumed birds and monkeys.

All these groups cross in front of the *bateria* of drummers filling the air with sound in the bull pen.

In da Costa's box, Jetta in particular wilts. Her greatly abbreviated costume of a Foreign Legionnaire looks hot and heavy over her breasts and hips. Her back leans against a stanchion. Her chin is on her chest. Her eyes are open, watching, but glazed.

The most important obligatory *ala* of any presentation is that which honors the earliest history of the samba parade in Rio de Janeiro. After the drought of 1877, women who had emigrated from Bahia danced slowly down the main street of Rio in their long white gowns on the Sunday before Lent, inviting the men to join them, as they had done in Salvador. So here comes the *Ala das Baianas*, scores of older women, usually the blackest in the favela, dressed, dancing in the flowing white robes of Bahia.

The *passistas* cause the greatest excitement and appreciation. Young people from the favela, the youngest fully formed girls and boys, the most beautiful and most handsome, clearly the most athletic, as near naked as possible without being cumbersomely nude, dance down the parade route together acrobatically, tumbling, doing cartwheels, climbing each other, leaping off, being caught by others a centimeter before disaster, all the while singing, of course, doing all this in a choreography so intricate, so closely timed it has taken them the full year to study it, learn it, practice it. Some of the young men may have developed a capoeira routine which is so graceful while so vicious, so rife with genuine danger, that the sight of it might stop the specta-tor's heart if the drums weren't controlling the heart, keeping it going.

Adrian Fawcett says something to Fletch.

Fletch yells, "What?" but cannot hear even his own voice.

Adrian cups his hands over Fletch's ear and yells with his full voice, virtually taking a full breath to blow out each word: "Think if all this energy, planning, work, skill the year 'round went into revolution instead!"

Fletch nods that he heard him.

Interspersed among the *alas*, a few *alegorias* have passed, huge floats depicting scenes from the Amazon, one a section of jungle bejeweled by women in G-strings suggesting plumed birds in their tall, bright, feathered headpieces; slim boys-men with the heads of snakes slithering over the rocks; children with the heads of monkeys dancing in the trees. Another *alegoria* depicts an Indian village, live fire centering thatched huts, costumed Indians dancing with mythical fish-headed and monster-headed figures.

In the middle of the presentation comes a small float, a disguised pickup truck, really a sound truck with amplifiers aiming every direction. On the back of the truck-float, dressed formally like a nightclub singer, stands the *Puxador de Samba*, microphone close to mouth, singing over and over at fullest personal volume, belting out the lyrics of the samba school's song for that year:

> Like the Amazon flows our history,
> Deep, mysterious and wide,
> Of many brooks and streams,
> Magically providing us with life.

After a few more *alas* does the *bateria* begin to pull out of the bull pen and join the parade. An entire army of drummers, perhaps a thousand or more powerful men from the ages of fifteen to whenever, uniformly dressed in dazzling costume, all beating their drums in patterns practiced all year, all singing, all dancing despite the size of their drums, pass by. The sound is overpowering. It is perhaps the maximum sound the earth and sky can accept without cracking, without breaking into fragments to move with it before dissipating into dust.

Near the end of the parade comes the samba school's principal *alegoria*. In this case, for Escola Guarnieri that year, a nineteenth-century riverboat slowly comes down the parade route, if not full-sized at least impressively huge—as white, as delicate, as ornate as a wedding cake. Its prow moves majestically down the street high above the heads of the *bateria*. The bridge is proud in its height. Steam comes from its funnels. The cap of its whistle funnel rises and lowers, and doubtlessly the sound of a steamboat whistle comes out, but so high is the level of sound generally that even a steamboat whistle cannot be heard fifteen meters away. The white, gleaming hull moves by slowly. The mere sight of the upper decks and into the interior cabins and ballroom of the ship instantly creates the feeling of a grander day, grander people, a grander way to travel, to move, to be. Sedately move the side wheels of this riverboat, exactly as if they were thrusting water behind them. And as the riverboat passes, its stern turned up to be high above the final dancing *ala* behind it, the last to disappear down the stream of swirling costumed dancers and drummers, instant yearning for it fills the heart, the instant and full desire to experience again the passing of this ghost, this *alegoria* of the past.

"I THINK YOU'RE GOING to have to tell me that there is life after Carnival," Fletch said.

At the bar table at the back of the box, Teo laughed and handed him a sandwich.

Other people were coming to the back of the box for drinks and sandwiches.

"Does everything become real again?" Fletch asked.

Adrian Fawcett said, "Reality has hunkered down somewhere in my gut, assumed the fetal position, and promises only in whispers to return."

The sound level had lowered to the merely very loud. Across the parade route, the *bateria* of Escola Santos Lima was organizing itself in the bull pen.

Jetta put her hand on Fletch's shoulder. "Are you supposed to be some kind of a present?"

She looked thoroughly sound-struck, sight-struck, mindblown, and jaded.

He smoothed his bright red sash.

"I'm a present," Fletch said. "Maybe I'm a past. Maybe I'm a future."

"And did you come *par avion*?"

Chewing, Teo said, "Did you and Laura come by subway?"

"Yes, Teo," Fletch said honestly. "Never have I seen an underground transportation system so modern, so quiet, so clean."

Dressed like a Christmas package and as an eighteenth-century musician, Fletch and Laura had ridden Rio's subway to

Carnival Parade at Teo's suggestion. Everyone had told them they could not get a car or a taxi within kilometers of Avenida Marquês de Sapucaí.

The ten-year-old Janio Barreto had followed Fletch and Laura from the Hotel Yellow Parrot to Avenida Marquês de Sapucaí.

In the subway station he ducked under the turnstile onto the platform. Fletch thought the underground official saw him, but the man took no notice. Who would keep a wooden-legged boy off public transportation because he had no money? On the train, Janio stood away from them, not looking at them, not speaking to them.

Fletch pointed him out to Laura, briefly told her about him.

She seemed particularly disturbed by being following by a small boy on a wooden leg.

Janio hobbled after them through the dark back streets to the Carnival Parade. At the entrance to the boxes he was stopped. Security was very heavy there, very official. Even with tickets, Fletch and Laura physically had to force, squeeze themselves through the bodies of the guards. They would not let anyone, even or especially a ten-year-old boy on a wooden leg, through the entrance to the boxes without a ticket.

"Yes." Fletch was aware Teo was watching his face. "A magnificent subway."

The Italian racing-car driver came to the bar table. "There are some Indians out there calling for you."

"Me?" Fletch asked.

The racing-car driver jerked his thumb over his shoulder, indicating the area beyond the box rail.

Laura was dancing in the center of the box with Aloisio da Silva. The heat had caused her leggings to drop over her patent leather shoes.

On the packed earth between the box and the pavement of

the parade route stood Toninho Braga, Orlando Velho, and Tito Granja. Again they were dressed as movie Indians. In that light, their shoulders and stomach ridges shone with sweat.

"Jump down!" Toninho shouted.

Fletch put perplexity on his face.

Cupping his hand over his mouth, Orlando shouted, "We need to talk to you!"

"Later!" yelled Fletch.

"About Norival!" shouted Toninho.

Tito waved his arm to encourage Fletch to jump down to them.

Fletch turned around.

Dancing with Aloisio, Laura's eyes were on Fletch's face.

Her own face was so expressionless it was unfathomable.

From behind him, Fletch heard the name *Janio* shouted.

He jumped the three meters from the box down to the Tap Dancers.

29

Toninho clapped Fletch on the shoulder. "You look Brazilian with that red sash. Probably just the way you did fifty years ago."

"Laura brought it to me from Bahia."

The four young men walked along the area between the boxes and the parade route.

Fletch said, "I was in a favela this morning. I don't see how the people in a favela can afford to put on such a presentation, all these drums and costumes and floats."

"It takes every cruzeiro, and then some," Toninho said. "By the way, I have lots of your money, your poker winnings, at my apartment. It's safe there. And dry."

"Thousands of beautiful costumes," Fletch mused. "Each must be individually made."

Tito said, "Everyone in a favela pays dues to the samba school every week. Also, the samba school gets some subsidy from the government for Carnival Parade. It's good for tourism."

"The *jogo do bicho*," Orlando said. "The *jogo do bicho* pays a lot."

"The illegal numbers game," Toninho said. "The people who run the illegal numbers games give a lot of money to the samba schools for Carnival Parade. It's their way of giving some of the money back, paying taxes—"

"Because they've been stealing from the people all year," Tito said. "Stealing their false hopes."

"It's good public relations for *jogo do bicho*," Tito said. "A business expense."

They had passed two or three of the judges' viewing towers.

Tito turned around and walked backwards. "Here comes Escola Santos Lima, Janio. Some of your descendants are parading."

"Escola Santos Lima has the best capoeiristas in all Rio de Janeiro," Orlando said. "Maybe all Brazil. A huge what-would-you-say squadron of them."

Toninho held Fletch's elbow. "Listen. Norival has not appeared."

"You miscalculated, Toninho. Miscalculated the currents. His body must have been carried out to sea."

"Not possible. Remember last night when I was swimming ashore? I swam into Norival. That proves that already he was floating toward the beach."

Against the noise of Carnival Parade the four young men held their heads close together as they walked.

"It would be terrible if Norival were eaten by a shark," Tito said.

"You don't see Norival as fish food?" Fletch asked.

"If it looks like he has just disappeared," Orlando asked practically, "how do we tell his family he is dead?"

"His poor mother," said Tito.

"His father will be awfully angry," said Toninho. "And Admiral Passarinho …"

"They will never forgive us for burying Norival at sea without them," Tito said.

"How would they ever believe us?" asked Toninho.

"You have a problem," Fletch admitted.

"The tide has been in and out and soon comes in again." Toninho looked sick. He looked as if the tide, with all its wiggly life, were passing through his own stomach and head.

"What do we do?" Orlando asked.

Fletch said, "Got me."

"What does that mean?"

"I haven't any idea."

"You are our friend, Fletch." Toninho still walked with Fletch's elbow in hand. "You helped us with Norival."

"Now you must help us think," said Tito.

"I don't think I can," said Fletch. "Someone I know who is alive has disappeared. Other people tell me I died forty-seven years ago and must name my murderer. I haven't slept. I am drunk with the sound of the drums. Norival has died and disappeared. Everything is becoming less real. How can I answer if I don't understand?"

They had walked half the length of the parade route.

Fletch stopped. "I must go back."

"Yes," said Tito. "He must see Santos Lima parade."

"You will tell us if you think of anything?" Toninho asked.

"Sure."

"Now we cannot fish the whole ocean hoping to catch the corpse of Norival," Orlando said.

"We'll telephone you," Toninho said. "Tomorrow, after the parade is over."

IF IT WERE NOT for his wounds, Fletch would have been willing to believe that finally he fell asleep and dreamed the most horrible dream.

As it was, later he was unsure of when he had been conscious and when he had been unconscious.

Dizzy with sleeplessness, having somewhat the sensation of intoxication from the constant sound of Carnival drums, perhaps staggering a little, alone he began to walk back along the parade route to Teodomiro da Costa's box. His eyelids were heavy, his vision diminished in that glaring light. The *Abra-Alas* of Escola Santos Lima passed by, the first *alegoria* reminding the spectators to expect a literary theme. The walk back to da Costa's box seemed as big a chore as crossing all Brazil on foot. He was aware of the passing of the *Commisão de Frente*. He stopped, swaying, trying to focus in the glare on the dancing of the *Porta Bandeira* and the *Mestre Sala*. Their dance steps were too quick, too intricate for him to follow with his eyes. At the first *ala*, he staggered forward again, only dimly aware of the passing of the thousands of dancing, singing people, the swirling costumes and flesh to his right.

Once back in Teo's box he would curl into a corner and sleep. For only an hour. People might be amazed or insulted at his sleeping during Carnival Parade, but he could not help it. He would arrange with Laura to wake him after an hour so people would not be too insulted. Even in that noise, he could, he had to sleep.

Just as he was comforting himself with this decision, using it to strengthen him to make it all the way back to Teo's box, strong hands pushed suddenly and hard against his left shoulder.

Instead of looking at who had pushed him, Fletch tried to save himself from falling. The edge of the parade route's pavement shot out from under him.

Someone pushed him again.

He fell to his right, into the parade.

A foot came up from the pavement and kicked him in the face.

Staggering from the blow, arms raised to protect his head, he looked around him. He was just inside the edge of perhaps a hundred young men doing their murderous, practiced kick-dancing. A foot landed flat against his stomach. Immediately, the air was gone from Fletch's lungs. Gasping, he tried to duck sideways, back to the edge of the parade.

Again he was pushed, hard.

Spinning, he fell more deeply into the group of capoeiristas. He was surrounded by fast-moving, swinging legs striking at crotch height, stomach height, shoulder height, head height. A blow landed against the back of his right knee. He fell against someone. All around him flashed intense eyes. *Aw, shit*, was in Fletch's head, *I'm messing up their presentation. A damned North American, a tourist.* He was being kicked from all sides. The eyes of the capoeiristas were seeing him, popping in amazement at his being there, but usually only after they had pirouetted, when it was too late for them to stop their momentum, avoid kicking him.

I don't belong here.

Someone had pushed him into the capoeira troupe, not just once but three times. Whoever pushed him doubtlessly was still between him and the edge of the parade. Arms over his head, Fletch ducked. Keeping as low as possible, he began to scurry across the parade route to the far side, toward the stands.

A hard kick in the stomach lifted him off his feet. He came down hard on his left foot. He kept moving forward, through the muscular bare backs shining with sweat, the wildly flailing legs, balancing arms. Without air or the ability to breathe, he felt he was drowning in an ocean of churning arms and legs. The sound of the drums, the sound of the men singing in short, practiced phrases, rushed in his ears. He was being kicked and kicked. Even the gray pavement of the parade route was heaving beneath his feet.

He didn't see the foot that came up from the pavement and

kicked him in his face. A cracking noise blasted his ears as his head snapped up and back.

A firm hand against his waist ejected him from the parade.

There was hard-packed earth beneath his feet. The capoeiristas were now a meter behind him.

Blood was on his hands. From his nose and ears and mouth blood was pouring down inside and outside his white shirt. It disappeared into his red sash.

He turned, half-conscious, to see if he could spot whoever had pushed him into the capoeira troupe.

The *Ala das Baianas* was passing by. A few of the tall black women in long white robes saw him, grimaced at his bloody appearance as they sambaed to the edge of the pavement and turned back.

His eyes wanted to close. He knew he had to go to ground somewhere.

Clutching his ribs, he turned toward the stands. A few people were pointing to him. Most were moving their heads, their shoulders to look beyond him, at the parade.

He staggered, fell toward the stands.

People he approached on the bottom tiers of seats stood up in horror at his appearance, to get away from him. Maybe one or two women were screaming. A few men were shouting at him, angrily, pointing at him. He could not hear the women screaming or the men shouting. He could only see their mouths move.

He knelt down and put his head and shoulders between the second and third tiers of seats. Whoever had pushed him into the capoeiristas had intended murder. Perhaps he had succeeded. Chances were good he would follow his quarry until he was sure he had killed him. His head under the seats, Fletch reached out, grabbed a couple of metal uprights and pulled himself through.

Fletch crawled beneath the stands.

He lay on his back on the dirt, the bottoms of the seats, the bottoms of the spectators just above him. He had been kicked in the stomach so many times he could not breathe.

Vomiting turned him over, got him up on his knees, got him gagging, breathing again. Blood from his nose and lips joined the more forceful stream of vomit.

On his knees, he backed away from his mess.

Stomach muscles quivering from the blows, arms and legs shaking, he remained on hands and knees coughing, trying to clear his throat of vomit and blood. A meter ahead of him, the people who had risen from their seats, allowing him to crawl under the stands, were sitting in their seats again, pounding their feet like pistons again in rhythm to the drums, cheering on the biggest and most amazing human spectacle in the world except war. Fletch knew they could not hear him retching and choking. He could not hear himself. He was sure his appearance to them was as unreal as the rest of the spectacle they were watching.

After a while he crawled backward farther to give himself more headroom, more air.

Sitting cross-legged then, he put his head back to try to stop the bleeding from his nose. He remembered the crack he had heard when he got that final kick in the face. He did not think his neck was broken, nor his back, nor his head.

Above him rose, as far as he could see, the undersides of the stands. Pieces of skirts, the undersides of thighs, a few dangling feet. A sandwich wrapper floated down and landed near him in the dirt.

The light under the stands was weird. It was midnight. There was no illumination under the stands. The powerful light from the parade route filtered under the stands through the densely packed bodies above. Nodes of light, apparently sourceless, quivered in midair.

Streams of light wavered at odd angles to each other.

His crotch hurt, his stomach hurt, his ribs. His head had been hit from every direction.

Fighting the temptation, his body's demand to stretch out, to go to sleep, become unconscious, he lifted himself to his feet. It took him three tries to become upright.

He fell forward, and caught himself. A *chope* can fell from the stands and landed near his foot. He put one foot forward and fell on it. Maintaining upright balance seemed important to him. One hand rubbed an ear; the other tightly held his ribs. He gasped.

Later, he supposed he had moments of unconsciousness as he stood there.

He saw a man walking along under the stands. About to wave to him, make some gesture he needed help, Fletch noticed how oddly the man walked. Fletch looked more closely. The man's steps were short, high, fast. He landed first on his toes and then his feet rolled forward to his heels.

The man's feet were backward. His toes were behind his legs.

The hand pressing against his ribs Fletch lowered to press against his stomach.

He blinked blood from his eyes.

A headless mule cantered out of the dark under the stands, slowly turned, and cantered away.

Fletch fell forward on his feet several steps. Now truly he was the walking North American, falling forward. Each step, his feet barely prevented his falling on his face.

Out of the dark at Fletch's left appeared another man, walking, bouncing slowly. He was to cross in front of Fletch.

As he passed Fletch, the man's head, backward on his shoulders, turned and smiled. His eyes and teeth shone even in that light.

In an impossible angle from his head, one of his arms raised. He pointed to Fletch's right.

Standing very close to Fletch was an old man in an oversized coat. The man's hair was thin and gray. His eyes were sad.

He raised his arms toward Fletch.

Fletch backed away.

Only hair came out of the old man's sleeves, not hands or wrists.

Again, Fletch's head snapped.

Someone kicked him hard, on the muscle of the upper left side of his back.

Brushing away the old man with hair for hands, Fletch spun slowly on the hard-packed earth.

He saw the second blow coming at his chest. He did not know how to avoid such a blow from the foot. He could not duck it. Moving sideways, slowly, stupidly, he still caught the full force of the blow.

His feet caught him as he fell backward.

A man, a wiry old man, was kick-dancing in front of him. Groggy, Fletch admired the perfectly executed pirouette.

And as the man's face turned to him, a beam of light through the stands shone fully on the face of a goat. Through the mask's eyeholes gleamed steady brown eyes.

The man's instep hit Fletch hard on the side of the head.

Fletch's head felt it was traveling through space by itself.

Reeling, Fletch saw the small boy standing not too far away on his wooden leg.

"Janio!" Fletch yelled. Blood bubbled from his throat to his lips.

In all that noise, he could not even hear his own voice.

His shoulders pumping unnaturally, the small boy ran away.

The capoeirista was real. He was in front of Fletch, behind him, all around him. The blows from his feet were real.

The man behind the goat mask was kicking Fletch to death.

Fletch tried to keep his legs together, yet not fall over. He tried to keep his back to the man, which was impossible. Hunkered down, he tried to keep his hands over his head, his elbows protecting his ribs. Falling this way, that, he tried to get away. The capoeirista was on all sides of him at once. Each blow from his feet opened Fletch's body for another blow.

Fletch received a hard kick in his throat, perhaps a killing kick.

Then one more kick in the back of his head.

He was face down in the dirt.

Consciousness was coming and going like an old song on a high wind. Blood was pouring from his face, particularly his nose again, but he could not get a hand to it.

His legs would not get him up. They would not obey orders, they were well beyond the necessary impulse to get up and run.

The man in the goat's mask grabbed Fletch's hair and twisted his head sideways and up. Fletch's whole body rolled sideways. He was lying on one hip.

A knee either side of him, the man knelt over Fletch.

For a second the man's hand was flattened on the ground in front of Fletch's nose. In one of the odd flashes of light, Fletch glimpsed a ring on the man's finger. A ring with a black center. Intertwined snakes rose from that center.

Farther along the ground, Fletch saw a piece of wood sticking into the ground again and again as it came closer. Paired with the stick of wood was a boy's leg.

Pulling Fletch's hair, the man in the goat mask twisted Fletch's head forward and back.

With his other hand, the man was doing something under Fletch's chin.

Fletch felt a nice warmth on the side of his neck.

The nice warmth of blood.

The man was slitting Fletch's throat.

Then, as if hit by a great wind, the man was blown sideways. He sprawled into the dirt beside Fletch.

Above them were many legs, strong men's legs.

In one incredibly smooth, lithe movement the man was up, on his feet, on one foot. The other foot on a straight leg was whirling through the air. From the ground, Fletch saw all the other legs, the legs of his rescuers, back away.

The toes of the man in the goat mask then dug into the ground with the grip of a sprinter. They were gone in a blur.

Heavily, the other feet went after him.

The wooden leg still stuck in the ground nearby, next to the boy's bare leg.

"Janio, I need help." On the ground, Fletch managed to get a hand to his throat. He stuck his finger in the knife hole. *"Janio! Socorro!"*

Fletch knew he was not being heard. He could not even hear himself.

It was not sleep then, into which Fletch fell.

30

He was conscious when the phone began ringing, but it rang five or six times before he could get rolled over, stretch his arm out to it, and pick up the receiver from the bedside table.

"*Bom dia*," Fletch said into the phone, not believing a word of it.

"Fletch! Are you better?"

By now, Fletch knew Toninho's voice over the telephone.

"Better than what?"

"Better than you were when we found you."

Fletch's memory was far from perfect. His brain had begun to clear only shortly before noon. He still tasted blood.

Lying on the ground under the stands at Carnival Parade, he remembered seeing from close-up the creases of Toninho's or Tito's belly.

He remembered being carried, it seemed for kilometers, under the stands. The sky was full of human feet and legs pounding in rhythm. The noise was no longer of singing, pounding samba drums. It was all just roar.

Then they were out from under the stands, and still he was

carried a long, long way. The sounds abated. The air became clearer. The sky was high and dark.

"We're getting good at lifting bodies around." Tito said. Why was he speaking English?

"Bury me at sea," Fletch instructed them. "The fish will appreciate dessert."

As they carefully fitted him into the back seat of the four-door black Galaxie, Fletch saw the ten-year-old boy standing next to the car. His eyes were round.

"Hey, Janio," Fletch said. "*Obrigado*."

During the ride in the car, he lost consciousness again. He remembered none of it.

He remembered being walked into the lobby of the Hotel Yellow Parrot. Orlando was holding him up.

The doorman and the desk clerk hurried around, each questioning Toninho and Tito in Portuguese. Toninho and Tito were placating.

The ride in the elevator took forever.

Finally, Fletch was on his own bed. Being on his bed was so unexpected, so wonderful, he sucked in great gobs of breath. And passed out again.

He remembered Toninho working up and down his naked body, squeezing, testing, looking for breaks in Fletch's bones.

"My neck," Fletch said. "Is my head on straight?"

Orlando came in from the bathroom with wet towels. He and Toninho washed Fletch down, even turning him over, gently, to do so.

As the towels passed in and out of Fletch's sight, they became pink, and then red.

The formally dressed desk clerk arrived with bandages and bottles of antiseptic.

He took away the wet, bloody towels and Fletch's blood-soaked clothes.

"Not my sash," Fletch complained. "Not my beautiful red sash."

"Your bloody red sash," Toninho said.

"Laura gave me that bloody red sash," Fletch said. "She brought it from Bahia."

"He says he'll burn your clothes," Tito said. "A sacrifice to the gods. They get only a little of your blood. You live."

"Ow."

Toninho was applying antiseptic to a hundred places over Fletch's body. He stuck the antiseptic-soaked face cloth into the small slit in Fletch's throat.

Consciousness was lost again.

They rolled Fletch this way and that, to put a fresh, dry sheet under him. The desk clerk was back in the room. He was trying to fold a wet, bloody sheet while not letting it touch his clothes.

With his fingers, Fletch discovered plaster stuck to various parts of his body: his shins, ribs, face, neck. He did not remember their being put on.

"Should I stay with him?" Tito asked.

"He'll be all right," Toninho said. "He needs a few hours of meditation. There's nothing really wrong with him."

"Except that someone tried to kill him," Orlando said.

"Yes," Toninho said. "It looks that way."

"He did not succeed," Fletch announced from the bed.

"No," Toninho said. "He did not succeed."

Softly, Tito said, "He almost succeeded."

The room was black. Fletch did not remember their leaving.

Through the dark night he listened to the samba drums. The sound was not coming from the street. It was coming from various televisions throughout the hotel, around the neighborhood. An announcer's voice came and went over the sound of the drumming and singing. Rio de Janeiro's Samba School Parade was continuing.

He did not sleep. Some unconsciousness other than sleep

came and went like a presence in the dark room. It came closer and went away.

He did not move. No part of his body wanted to move. Every muscle in his body had been kicked at least once. The skin and tissue against his bones throbbed. For a while, the thighs of his legs would hurt; he would think about them, then his shoulders; and he would think about them, his back, the area high in his stomach just below his ribs. Even his fingers and toes hurt. Anything was better than thinking how his head hurt. His head felt as if the inside had been kicked loose from the outside and rattled.

Laura would return. Sometime during the morning. Or perhaps within an hour after the parade was over, by two or three in the afternoon. How could she know, at the parade, he had been kicked almost to death? All she knew was that he had left the box to take a walk with the Tap Dancers. She would return.

Daylight came through the balcony drapes. Then direct sunlight entered the room. The television coverage of Carnival Parade continued. The room grew hot.

In his bed he experimented moving an arm. Then the other. One leg. He dug his fingers into his left leg to cause it to move. Slowly, he rolled his head back and forth on the pillow.

His head was clearing. He had not been unconscious for a long time now.

It was nearly noon when he could resist no longer.

Slowly he rolled himself to the edge of the bed. Heavily he lifted himself up. The semidark room went out of focus for a minute. He took a step forward. There was no part of his body which did not hurt.

After using the toilet, he turned on the bathroom light and looked at himself in the mirror. To his regret, his head was on frontwards and stared back at him. Swollen eyes, bruised cheekbones, jaws. One ear was inflamed. There was still blood in his hair. A shower would cause his bandages to fall off. Backing up, he saw the blue bruises on his upper arms, his chest. The top of his stomach was purple.

Brushing his teeth gingerly, he spat blood into the basin.

Then he returned to bed and waited.

Laura would come and they would have food. He would tell her what had happened to him. Would she listen? What had happened to him? Would she be interested, or would this be a level of reality which didn't interest her much? While he talked, would she be hearing something else? As he was leaving the box to join the Tap Dancers, her face had been inscrutable. What did the fact of the wooden-legged boy following them through the subway mean to her it did not mean to him?

Laura had not returned by the time Toninho called.

"You must be better," Toninho said. "You've had almost twelve hours to meditate."

"I need twelve years."

"Who tried to kill you?"

"I'm thinking about that."

"Ah, Carnival," Toninho said.

"He was wearing a goat mask," Fletch said. "A man in his sixties, I'd say. He tried to kick me to death."

"He must have slipped into the personality of the goat. Carnival does that."

"No goat has such training in capoeira." Fletch wanted to switch the phone to his other ear. Then he remembered his other ear had slipped into the personality of a tomato.

"The news is that Norival has showed up."

"Great! In one piece?"

"Yes. He came ashore way down the coast, a hundred kilometers south of where we thought."

"I always thought that boy would go a long way."

"Apparently he got caught in a current, which took him south, then ashore. He was on the beach this morning. A jogger found him. They are bringing his body up now."

"Good. Great. All your worries are over."

"The report so far is that he drowned. His boat broke up and he drowned."

"That's good. So Norival did die at sea. His mother will be so glad. Admiral Passarinho will be ecstatic."

"So we'll see you at the funeral home in about a half an hour."

"What? No way. Toninho, I can't move."

"Of course you can move."

"Why should I go to the funeral home?"

"To help us distract the officials." Toninho's voice fell to the conspiratorial. "To distract them from any idea of an autopsy. We need to stand around in a circle and say, yes, he drowned. We saw him go sailing and indeed he certainly did drown. They're more apt to believe you, you see. They don't know you as well as they know us."

"I don't think I can move."

"You must move. If you don't make yourself move now, you'll stiffen up, like Norival, and not be able to move for days."

Fletch hesitated. He remembered past injuries. "You're probably right."

Still, he had had no real sleep.

"Of course I'm right. The funeral home of Job Pereira. On Rua Jardim Botanico. The business part of the road."

"I'll find it."

"I'll bring all your gambling winnings to you."

"You needn't bribe me." Fletch tried sitting up in bed. "On the other hand, maybe you do."

31

At the funeral home of Job Pereira, Fletch tried to find a doorbell to ring, a door on which to knock. There was neither.

It was a large stucco and stone house sitting in the deep shade of its own trees.

"Hello?" he called. "Anyone?"

The quiet from inside the building was tomb-like.

He stepped into the coolness of the foyer. There was no reception desk, still no bell to ring. There were short, dark potted palms in each corner.

"Hello?" Fletch called.

The only response was a faint echo of his own voice.

It had taken him longer than the promised half hour to get from the Hotel Yellow Parrot to the funeral home of Job Pereira.

Sitting on the edge of his bed, he had ordered food from room service.

While still at the telephone, he called the Hotel Jangada and asked for Room 912.

No answer.

No, Mrs. Joan Collins Stanwyk had not yet picked up the envelope Mr. Fletcher had left in her box.

Every step, every movement, however small, caused him pain. He opened the drapes to the balcony. Across the utility area, the man was painting the room. Perhaps the man's permanent job in life was to paint that room. Fletch opened the door to the balcony. The air was warm and dry and felt good. The televisions were still blaring the news of Carnival Parade.

Life goes on.

Shaving was like walking barefoot through a field of glass. Finished, he had to affix one more bandage to his face.

Alone, with stinging lips and sore jaws, he ate breakfast.

Every minute, he thought Laura might return.

Finally dressed in a pair of clean shorts and a T-shirt, sneakers and socks, he went down in the elevator. The desk clerk and the few other people in the lobby glanced at him and immediately looked away. Despite the glue stuck to various parts of his face and body, he gathered he no longer looked like a Christmas package.

The avenida in front of the hotel was emptier than he had ever seen it. Citizens either were still watching Carnival Parade or were worn out by it and sleeping.

Finally a taxi picked him up. All the streets were empty. All the way to the funeral home, the taxi radio kept up an excited description of the last *escola* to parade.

"Hello? Anyone here?"

The funeral home was lifeless. There was not even the sound of a radio or television reporting the parade.

Fletch limped into a big room to the left of the foyer. Heavy, waisted velvet drapes on the windows cut down the light in the room.

Several open coffins were on display in the room. Each was on its own fancy trestle. He looked in one. It was empty. A coffin sales room. He moved from coffin to coffin, looking in each. The coffins ranged from polished pine to brass-studded mahogany.

He heard a sound behind him.

A seemingly tired, lazy voice said, "Hello?"

Fletch turned around.

In the door to the room, white as sea foam, the brighter light from the foyer behind him softening his outline, clearly stood Norival.

Norival Passarinho.

Dressed in white shoes, white slacks, white shirt. His belly hung over his belt. Damp hair fell onto his forehead. His face was puffy.

Norival Passarinho!

Fletch blinked.

Norival blinked.

Fletch sucked in cool air from the coffin display room.

"Ah, Janio Barreto." Norival shambled toward Fletch. Norival even put out his arm to take Fletch's hand. "At last I get to meet you properly!"

The room rose.

Fletch fell.

32

Fletch knew he was in a small, dark place.

Becoming conscious, he could hear no natural sounds except the sound of his own breathing. The air was stale.

He was lying on his back. His head was on some kind of pillow.

Only when he moved his right hand and immediately came to the edge of the space, a soft wall, did he realize how small the space was. The same was true when he moved his left hand.

The space he was in clearly was no wider than a long, narrow bed. He ran his hands up the satiny walls. The ceiling of the space was immediately on top of him, only a few centimeters above his chest, his chin, his nose.

A very small space indeed.

His fingers brushed against something else. Paper, fairly stiff paper. Both hands felt over the object lying beside him in the small space. His fingers told him it was a paper bag, with papers in it.

Fletch tried to think where he had last been, what had happened to him, at what he had been looking when … Coffins!

"Aaaaaaaaarrrgh!" Fletch's roar surprised and deafened himself. "I'm not dead?"

In that terrible enclosure, he tried to get his hands up, to press up, raise the lid of the coffin. His heart was pounding in a lively manner. His face poured sweat.

"Hey, out there!"

Horrified, he realized he might be trying to yell through six feet of sod.

"Hey, up there! I'm not dead yet! I swear to it!"

He could not get his arms, hands at the right angle to lift. The coffin lid was heavy. His beaten muscles quivered and ached but accomplished little.

"Aaaaaaaaarrrgh! Somebody! Anybody! Listen! I'm not dead yet!" The air in the coffin had become exceedingly warm. "*Socorro!* Damn it!"

By itself, it seemed, the coffin lid rose.

Instantly, the air became fresh and sweet.

He blinked stupidly at the light of day.

Laura's head was over the coffin, looking in. "Ah, there you are," she said.

Lying flat, sucking in the good air, Fletch said nothing.

"What are you doing in a coffin?"

Fletch panted.

"You do look like you belong in a coffin."

"I saw Norival," he said. "Norival Passarinho."

"Norival's dead," she said.

"I know!"

"Apparently he went sailing alone at night. His boat hit a rock or something. He drowned."

"I know!"

"His body washed up this morning. Very sad. Poor Norival."

"I know all that, Laura. But, listen! I came here to the funeral home. Toninho asked me to. I was alone, in this room." Fletch peered over the edge of his coffin and established that he was still in the coffin display room. "And I turned around, and there, in the door, stood Norival! Norival Passarinho! Blinking!"

"Norival?"

"He spoke to me! He said, 'Janio Barreto.' He came forward. He walked across the room at me. He tried to shake my hand!"

Laura wrinkled up her nose. "Norival Passarinho?"

"Yes! Definitely!"

"After he was dead?"

"Yes! I know he was dead!"

"It couldn't have been Norival Passarinho."

"It was Norival Passarinho. Dressed in white. All in white."

"You saw Norival Passarinho walking around after he was dead?"

"He said, Norival said, 'Ah, Janio Barreto.'" Fletch lowered his voice to the sepulchral. "'At last I get to meet you properly.'"

"You saw Adroaldo Passarinho."

"What? Who?"

"Adroaldo. Norival's brother. They're just alike."

Fletch thought a moment. "Adroaldo?"

"Yes. Adroaldo was very surprised when he put out his arm to shake hands with you, and you fainted."

"I fainted?"

"Well, you fell on the floor without apparent what-do-you-call-it? premeditation."

"Adroaldo Passarinho?"

"You didn't know Norival had a brother?"

"Yes. Of course. But he was so white!"

"He's been in school in Switzerland all winter."

"Laura…"

"Fletch, I think you're not surviving Carnival. It's beginning to affect your mind."

"What am I doing in a coffin?"

Laura shrugged. "I suspect the Tap Dancers put you in there. After you fainted."

"Why?"

"One of their little tricks." She giggled.

"Very funny!" Stiffly, he began to pull himself up, to sit up in his coffin. "God! I thought …"

"It is funny."

He picked up the paper bag and looked into it.

"What's that?" she asked. "Your lunch? Enough to tide you over to the other world?"

"My poker winnings."

"Ah, they buried you with all your worldly wealth. All your ill-gotten gains. So you can tip Charon after he rows you across the River Styx."

His time in the coffin had stiffened his muscles again. "How come you're here?"

"Toninho called me at the hotel. Said you had fainted. I should come in the car and pick you up. Adroaldo and the others had to go with Norival in his coffin to the Passarinho home."

Fletch's heart had slowed, but he was still sweating. "What if you hadn't come? I could have run out of air—"

"Why wouldn't I have come?"

"Supposing the car had broken down, or—"

"You could have gotten yourself out of there."

"I could have died of cardiac arrest."

"Were you that frightened?"

"Waking up in a closed coffin is not something one expects to do—under any circumstances."

She was studying his face. "You're a mess."

"I got nearly kicked to death."

"They told me. Your whole body like that?"

"At the moment, I am not very sleek."

"Was there any reason for it you know of? I mean, getting attacked?"

"I think so, yes. Help me out of this damned coffin, if you don't mind."

"Also, there was another message for you at the hotel." She balanced him by holding onto his hand. "A Sergeant Paulo Barbosa of Rio de Janeiro police would like you to call him."

"What did he say?"

"Just left a message. How much trouble are you in?"

"Oh, my God." A body wounded in every part is painful to lift out of a raised coffin and set on two feet on the floor.

"You really are a mess," Laura said. "The car is just outside."

"You'd better drive."

"Seeing the last vehicle you tried to drive is a coffin …"

"Not by choice, thank you."

"We'll go back to the hotel. The Parade is over. It was really wonderful. You missed most of it."

"I'm sorry about that."

"Fletch, you always seem to be someplace you're not supposed to be, doing something you're not supposed to be doing."

"Got any other news for me?"

"Yes." They were crossing the wide, cool foyer of the funeral home of Job Pereira, heading for the dazzling sunlight beyond the front door. "Paul Bocuse is the chef at Le Saint Honoré. I've made reservations for tonight, in your name. Have you forgotten the ball at Regine's? That's tonight. Tomorrow, I thought we'd drive up and have a quiet lunch at Floresta."

"You mean Carnival still isn't over?"

"Tomorrow night it's over. I'm not at all sure you'll make it. I'll have to start preparing for my concert tour soon enough. Not a worry. We'll go back to the hotel and rest now."

"No."

"No? You want to go play soccer now?"

"I want to go to favela Santos Lima now." Over the top of the small yellow convertible, she gave him a long look. "I'll never rest until I do. You said so yourself."

"I don't think I know the way."

"I do." He lowered himself gently onto the hot passenger seat. "Just follow my directions."

33

Sore with wounds, dazed with sleeplessness, Fletch walked into favela Santos Lima like a *Figura de Destaque*. The sun was searingly, blindingly hot.

Laura traipsed along a few steps behind him.

The children of the favela followed him too, of course, but they walked at a distance from him, quietly. As they climbed the hill, adults from the little houses and the little shops followed them.

By the time they were in front of Idalina Barreto's house, they were a large crowd.

The tall old woman recognized Laura immediately. Hands on her hips in the doorway of her little house, she began talking to Laura even before Laura got to the front of the house. The old woman asked, repeated some question of Laura.

The crowd outside the house was quiet. They wanted to hear Fletch's answer.

Laura said, "She wants to know if you've come to identify your murderer."

Fletch said, "I think so. Tell her I think so."

Laura frowned. "Are you serious?"

"Is anything serious?"

"How do you mean to do that?"

"I mean to walk slowly through the favela, look into every-one's eyes. I shall identify my murderer."

"Just like that?"

"Just like that."

"I don't believe ..." She looked around at all the people quietly awaiting Fletch's response.

"What don't you believe?" he asked. "What do you believe?"

Fletch waited a long time for her to answer. He asked, "Would you like to believe I'm about to perform magic? That I'm about to do a trick?"

Still Laura did not answer.

"Would you like to believe, as some of these people do, that I am Janio Barreto returned from the dead after forty-seven years to point out my murderer?"

"I believe ..." In the heat of the sunlight, Laura took a deep breath. "I don't believe you should play with these people."

"Am I playing?"

"At least some of these people believe this story. Because the old lady wants them to believe. The others are just curious. They love any story."

"Anybody can make up a story and say it is the past. Right?"

"Identifying someone as your murderer, as the murderer of Janio Barreto, would be a very serious thing for these people."

"I hope so."

"You have no idea what they might do to such a person."

"I can guess."

"Fletch, you must tell me what you know."

"You want a fact?"

"I want something."

"Okay, Laura, here's a fact: The person who murdered Janio

Barreto forty-seven years ago truly believes I am Janio Barreto returned."

"How do you know that?"

"Look at me."

"I don't think you should play with the, what's-the-word? credibility of people."

"I am taking advantage of the credulity of only one of these people."

"Someone believes—"

"Someone either believes I am Janio Barreto returned. Or he has decided to act as if he believes I am Janio Barreto returned, just in case it is true."

In the sunlight, Laura sighed.

Now there were even more people standing around outside Idalina Barreto's house awaiting his answer.

The child Janio Barreto had appeared. Of all the people in the favela, he stood closest to Fletch.

"Please tell the old woman I am here to identify my murderer."

Laura started to speak to Idalina, but then stopped.

Instead, she said to Fletch: "You're putting it to me too, aren't you?"

"Hell, Laura, we haven't even gotten to know each other."

"All this will be on your head," she said.

"Fine. My head is so sore now, it doesn't matter."

Speaking loudly, as if making an announcement, Laura answered the old woman.

The crowd cheered. Many gave the thumbs-up sign.

The old woman asked another question.

Laura said, "Do you really mean to just walk through the favela, up and down the streets, until you point someone out?"

"I want to see, to look into the eyes of everyone in the favela. Tell her, if the murderer is here, I will find him."

Laura translated, in a less robust voice.

Idalina Barreto came out of the shade of her doorway.

In the sunlight, she took Fletch's arm.

Together, Laura walking behind them, the people from the favela all around them, Fletch and Idalina Barreto began to walk through favela Santos Lima.

"I KNOW YOUR TRICK," Laura finally said to Fletch in a low voice. They had been walking a long time. Her hair had collapsed with perspiration. "You're going to walk through the whole favela and point no one out."

"Maybe," Fletch answered. "Would that permit me to sleep?"

Favela Santos Lima was far more extensive than he thought. It was a senseless warren of streets and alleys and footpaths. The banged-together, stuck-together hovels seemed placed by the whimsy of the moment, or some invisible convenience. On some of the paths only he and Idalina could walk abreast. The stream of their followers flowed a kilometer behind them in some places.

"We're having our own Carnival Parade," Fletch said to Laura.

"Not bloody likely."

Sweating, the middle-aged Janio Barreto Filho appeared and asked what was happening. His mother told him *Janio Barreto* wished to look into the eyes of everyone in the favela. He would identify his murderer.

Janio Barreto Filho organized boys and men to walk ahead of Fletch and Idalina and get all the people out of their homes so Fletch could look into their eyes as he passed.

It was the afternoon after the Samba School Parade, and most of the people in the favela were sleeping. Barreto's squad called through the windows of their homes, entered, awakened people, and politely asked them to come outside. *No, no, it is not the police. It is an important matter. To solve an ancient matter having to do with the favela. We are about to find out who murdered Janio Barreto, a long time ago.* Shy of most clothes, faces puffy with tiredness, the people stood at their doors rubbing their eyes in the sunlight.

Perhaps they understood a feat of legerdemain was about to happen: a voice from beyond the grave was about to speak. Perhaps they understood nothing but that someone had asked them to wake up and stand outside a moment. Something interesting was passing by. Sleepy or curious, they cooperated.

Fletch asked Laura, "Are you deciding what you believe now?"

"All these people." Laura looked back at the river of people following them. "Many of them are laughing at you."

"I would hope so," he said.

"Turning this into a joke. Is that what you're doing?"

"Isn't it a joke?"

"You're going to lead them around in a circle and then say there is no such person as your murderer here."

"Perhaps."

As he walked, Fletch was becoming less stiff. He was thirsty. The sun was stinging his various wounds on his face and arms. His head throbbed like a samba combo. A few times, the bright sunlight dimmed on him unnaturally. He stumbled. Idalina Barreto's grip on his arm was strong.

Of course he did not know if he was going up and down every path in Santos Lima. He had to leave that to his guides. It certainly felt as though he was going up and down every path, looking into the eyes of every person in Santos Lima.

"I'm going back," Laura said. "Here are the car keys. I'll take a taxi."

"No," said Fletch. "Stay with me."

"I don't care to see out the end of this act of yours."

"It's not an act."

Fletch was seeing the people of favela Santos Lima. He was seeing males and females, the old, the young, the tall, the short, the beautiful, the ugly, the misshapen, the healthy, the insane, the doddering, the dignified, the ashamed …

Ahead of him on a narrow path, he saw a lean, gray-haired man dressed only in shorts leave a house. He crossed the path and entered another house.

Walking more quickly, Fletch approached that house.

In excitement, Idalina Barreto gripped his arm even tighter. She kept up with him.

Young Janio Barreto looked up into Fletch's eyes. Then, calling others, he ran ahead and into the house.

Fletch entered the house. It was empty. There was a doorless back door.

From behind the house came the sound of young Janio Barreto calling loudly.

As Fletch went through the house, the mob following gathered speed. They went through the house and round the house.

Now they had the idea they were pursuing someone.

"What are you doing?" Laura said. "Madman!"

Fletch looked back. A wall of the little house they had just gone through fell flat in the dust. The other three walls fell forward but did not collapse. The twisted tin roof kept three of the walls up.

"You're out of your mind!" Laura said. "There is no understanding this!"

Above the little house he came to a wider path. To his left down the path, young Janio Barreto held onto the black shorts of the gray-haired man he knew Fletch was pursuing. Other boys, men, surrounded the man.

More slowly now, Fletch walked toward the group in the middle of the path.

As he approached, one of the young men said to the gray-haired man, "Just let him look into your eyes, Gabriel."

"*Gabriel Campos!*" Idalina Barreto shrieked in her highest crone's voice. "*Gabriel Campos!*"

Clearly the man wanted to bolt. He was surrounded now by twenty strong young men, by more than thirty children. He was being approached by more than one hundred fellow citizens of his favela.

With dignity, he stood his ground. His body was mostly light, sinewy muscle. The top of his stomach was pumping hard. The man had not moved that far, not moved that fast, to be so out of breath. Not for a man in his condition. A disingenuous smile played on his lips.

"*Gabriel Campos!*" Idalina shrieked. Then she shouted something about Janio Barreto.

Standing close to him, Fletch looked into the eyes of Gabriel Campos. He had seen those eyes before.

Gabriel Campos' eyes flickered. He looked at the crowd and back at Fletch.

His smile came and went like a flashing light.

Slowly, Fletch raised his hand.

He pointed his index finger at Gabriel Campos' nose.

Fletch already had checked the ring the man was wearing. It had a black center. Intertwined snakes rose from that center.

Instantly, Gabriel Campos ducked. Throwing back his elbows, he darted backward through the circle of young men, children, knocking over a child.

Idalina Barreto shrieked.

Others began to yell, move forward.

Two of the young men grabbed for Gabriel Campos.

Campos kicked one in the stomach; the other in the face.

It seemed everyone was trying to lay a hand on Campos.

With tremendous skill, ducking and dancing, he kicked free of the crowd.

He turned and ran up the path.

Shouting, young men ran after him. Tripping over each other, almost all the men and children who had been following Fletch joined the pursuit. Yelling, some lifting their skirts up, many of the women pursued Gabriel Campos as well.

Shrieking *Gabriel Campos! Gabriel Campos!* tall old Idalina Barreto went after him in her rapid, sturdy pace, losing ground in the midst of this marathon.

Fletch sat on a nearby rock.

Dor de estomago … de cabeca … febre … nausea.

A FEW METERS AWAY, Laura Soares was in a group of women from the favela. They were all talking at once. Most of them were pregnant and therefore could not join in the pursuit of Gabriel Campos.

Laura was asking questions. She kept looking across at Fletch.

Higher up in the favela, the chase was still going on. On a road along a ridge, Fletch saw Gabriel Campos running between the houses. Easily one hundred people were streaming after him. He had a good lead on them.

Idalina Barreto's high, shrill shriek dominated all other sounds. "Gabriel Campos! Gabriel Campos!"

FROM SOMEWHERE DOWN in the depths of the favela came the sound of a samba drum.

After a while, Laura came over to Fletch. She stood over him a moment without speaking.

Fletch said, "I'm awfully tired. And I still have to call Sergeant Barbosa of the Rio police."

Laura said, "His name is Gabriel Campos."

"I heard." He looked up to where Idalina Barreto was. The old lady had climbed far fast. "I hear."

"The women say he was your friend when you were boys. He, one other boy, and the Gomes brothers. Who are the Gomes brothers?"

"Idalina's brothers."

"See?" she said. "You do know."

"I was told, Laura. Yesterday. I was told."

"You taught them all the skill of capoeira. Of everyone, Gabriel learned the best. After you were killed, he was master of the capoeira school of Escola Santos Lima. For years, he was famous for it. One year, he was even *Mestre Sala*."

"I see. He wanted Janio—his teacher—out of the way."

"He was placed on the board of directors of the samba school."

"He would never have had such honors if Janio were alive."

Laura made some sign in the dust with the tip of her sandal.

"I must get sleep." High in the favela, the pursuit, the shouting continued. Fletch said, "I wonder what they will do with him."

"I don't want to know. How, why did you pick out Gabriel Campos? You must tell me."

"You mean, did Gabriel Campos murder Janio Barreto forty-seven years ago?"

"Did he?"

"I don't know." Beyond exhaustion, Fletch stood up from the rock. "But I do know that, disguised as a goat, last night he tried to slit my throat."

34

"I forget if you said if you have ever been to New Bedford, Massachusetts." Sergeant Paulo Barbosa asked.

"No," Fletch said into the phone. He sat heavily on his bed in the Hotel Yellow Parrot. "I have never been to New Bedford, Massachusetts."

Laura had gotten Sergeant Barbosa on the line. Placing the call had seemed too complicated to Fletch in his sleepless condition.

"It is very nice in New Bedford, Massachusetts," Sergeant Barbosa told him again. "Much too cold, of course, for me. When you go back to your country, you must visit New Bedford, Massachusetts." Fletch noticed the presumption that sooner or later everyone does go back to his country. It was the same presumption Idalina's father made of Janio Barreto. "You must visit my cousin's gift shop in New Bedford, Massachusetts. She has everything in her gift shop that every other gift shop has."

"All right." Fletch's head was nodding. "I promise."

"That would be very nice. Now, about that North American woman you lost ..."

Fletch's eyes popped open. "Yes?"

"I don't think we have found her."

"Oh."

"What we have is a telephone call from the mayor of a very small town on the coast, south of here three hundred kilometers. The town of Botelho. It is very nice there. Very sealike. It is on the ocean. You should visit there anyway."

"Yes," Fletch said drowsily. "I'll visit there, too. I promise I will."

Laura was pulling the drapes closed against the sunlight. She had already stripped for bed.

"The mayor of Botelho said that on the weekend, Saturday, I think it was, a North American woman showed up there in Botelho."

"Perhaps somebody told her she should visit."

"Very likely. It is a nice place. I have taken my wife and children there."

"Did you have a nice time?"

"A very nice time."

"Good."

"The mayor said this woman just wandered around for the afternoon by herself, on the beach and so forth, you know?"

"An American tourist—"

"After dark, she went into the very excellent seafood restaurant they have there. I brought my wife and children to eat there."

Kneeling before him, Laura was taking off Fletch's sneakers and socks.

"Was it good?"

"Excellent. This woman ate her dinner."

"A North American woman tourist went to a small resort town—"

"Botelho."

"Botelho, yes. Spent the afternoon on the beach and then had dinner in a seafood restaurant."

"Yes, that's right. After dinner, she said nothing. Instead of paying she went straight into the kitchen and began washing dishes."

Laura pushed Fletch onto his back and began taking off his shorts.

"That's not Joan Collins Stanwyk."

"She's been there ever since. Two days. Washing dishes. Eating. The man who owns the restaurant has given her a little bed to use."

"Joan Collins Stanwyk never washed a dish in her life. She wouldn't know how."

"She is a blond North American or English lady. She speaks no Portuguese."

"How old is she?"

Kneeling over him on the bed, Laura was taking off his shirt. The telephone wire went through the sleeve.

"Quite young, the mayor says. Slim. In her twenties. Maybe her midtwenties."

"Sounds to me like some female derelict from the Florida Keys washed up on a Brazilian beach."

"Botelho. The beach is very nice there."

"I'm sure." Laura was sliding Fletch's legs under the sheet. "Why did the mayor of Botelho call the Rio police about this lady?"

"Saturdays a tour bus from Copacabana hotels stops in Botelho. The mayor thought she might have gotten off the bus. So he called this police station. He asked if we were looking for a murderess of her description."

"A murderess?"

"Truth, he doesn't know where she came from. Or why. Botelho is a small town. He is a small mayor."

Finally in his bed, to sleep, Fletch thought a moment. Then he said, "I don't think so, Sergeant. Joan Collins Stanwyk didn't have any cash on her, but she is a wealthy, responsible lady, a lady of great dignity. She has many options open to her. All the options in the world. I can't see her ever going to a resort and getting a job washing dishes in a fish-and-chips joint."

"Fish-and-chips? Ah, you are speaking London English."

"Anyway, Joan Collins Stanwyk is in her thirties."

"I didn't think this would be the lady."

"I'm sure it's not."

"Topsy-turvy. Do you remember what I said about topsy-turvy?"

"In fact, I do."

"This is a very topsy-turvy world. Twenty-seven years I have served with the Rio police. Believe me, I have seen topsy-turvy."

"I'm sure you have. Thanks for being in touch with me, Sergeant."

Laura was in the bed beside Fletch.

"So," she said, "they have not found the woman you are looking for."

"No. Just some English-speaking woman has showed up washing dishes in some fish restaurant down the coast."

Into the dark, Laura said, "The police just want you to think they are doing something about the disappeared lady."

"Probably." He turned on the bedside light.

"What are you doing?"

"Just calling the Hotel Jangada," Fletch said. "See if she has returned."

"Want me to help you?"

"This one I can do myself," he said. "I've been practicing."

At the Hotel Jangada, Room 912 did not answer.

The desk clerk said Mrs. Joan Collins Stanwyk had not checked out.

Nor had she picked up the note Fletch had left for her.

Fletch—

I could not wake you up.

I tried and tried. A few times I thought you were awake, because you were talking. What you said made no sense. Did you know you talk in your sleep?

You said you were on a big white riverboat, and the sky was full of buttocks.

You said you had your goat, or someone was trying to get your goat. You seemed afraid of a kicking goat. Then, remarkably, you babbled on about an ancient Brazilian mythical figure, the dancing nanny goat.

How do you know about such things? Sometimes, when you were talking in your sleep, your eyes were open, which is why I thought I was succeeding in waking you. You said something about a man with his feet turned backward, another mythical figure, and when I asked, "Fletch, do you mean the capoeira?" you just stared off like some sort of a *almapenada*, a soul in torment. You also mentioned other

Brazilian hobgoblins, the man with his head on backward, the headless mule, and the goblin with-hair-for-hands. You talked about being pursued by a one-legged boy, and when I asked, "Fletch, do you mean the *Saci-perêrê*?" you stared a long time before saying, "Janio Barreto ... Janio Barreto ..."

Amazing thing is, you didn't know the names of any of these Brazilian scary figures. You seemed to be seeing them in some sort of a nightmare. You were sweating profusely. Do you think you had a fever? I am amazed you have such bad dreams of such hobgoblins, like a Brazilian child, when you have never heard of them or read of them, as far as I know.

Later, when I tried again to wake you, you said, "Leave the dead alone!"

Maybe you frightened me. A little.

I canceled our reservation for dinner at Le Saint Honoré. I gave our tickets to the ball at Regine's to Marilia, who gave them to some people she knows from Porto Alegre.

Your body is a real mess.

I decided what you need is rest.

I have gone back to Bahia. Carnival is almost over, for this year. I must start organizing my music for the concert tour.

Perhaps you would come to Bahia and advise me of what music you think should be included in the program.

Now maybe my father will be interested in talking to you—now that he knows you have studied up on such things as the *boitatá* and the *tutu-marambá*!

Ciao,
Laura

Fletch had awakened into bright sunlight. He was very hungry. He was very stiff. His body was sticky with sweat.

For a long moment, he thought it was still Monday afternoon and the sun had not yet set.

"Laura?" The hotel room was totally quiet. There was no noise from the bathroom. "Laura?"

From the bed, he noticed that her cosmetics, all those bottles which issued smells if not beauty, were gone from the bureau. None of her clothes were around the room. Her suitcase was gone from the rack.

His watch was on the bedside table. It read five minutes past eleven. Even in a topsy-turvy world, the sun did not shine brightly at five minutes past eleven on Monday nights.

Slowly it dawned on him it must be five minutes past eleven Tuesday morning.

He had slept seventeen hours.

Having to ask individually each part of his body to move, he got up from his bed and walked across the room.

Instead of Laura's cosmetics on the bureau was Laura's letter.

He read it twice.

Had he really talked so much in his sleep, said all those things to Laura? What's a *boitatá* and a *tutu-marambá*? Indeed, he must have frightened her.

Vaguely, he remembered having bad dreams. The boy, Janio Barreto, was following them down that crowded, dark slum street to Carnival Parade. In bright floodlights, Fletch was hunkered down in a swirling mass of bodies, brown eyes popping in surprise at seeing him there, being kicked from every direction. Again he was under the stands at Carnival, where he did not belong, looking through his own blood at a man walking by slowly, his head on backward, turning to smile at him ...

In the bathroom, he tore the bandages off himself. Scabs had formed nicely. Red marks had turned purple, and purple marks had turned black.

Hadn't Laura seen the big white riverboat floating sedately down the stream of swirling costumes? Hadn't that been real?

Gingerly, adding no more cuts to his face, Fletch shaved.

Janio Barreto following them through the subway to Carnival Parade had meant something to Laura it had not meant to him. What had her letter said? *Saci-perêrê*. What's a *saci-perêrê*?

The warm water of the shower felt good on his body. The soap did not feel so good on some of his wounds.

In fact, Laura had not really asked him what happened to him under the stands at Carnival Parade. She thought anyone can tell a story and say it is the past. Even after his pointing out Gabriel Campos at Santos Lima, she did not really ask. She only asked how, why he pointed out Gabriel Campos.

He did not dry himself after the shower. Instead, he just wrapped the towel around his waist. The air felt too good on his wet body.

His mind a jumble, he went out onto the balcony. A small samba combo was playing, probably outside a nearby café. Across the utility area, the man was still painting the room.

Laura thought it was funny the Tap Dancers had left him in a closed coffin with his bag of money. He had seen Norival Passarinho walk after he was dead. On broomsticks, his ankles tied to the ankles of Toninho and Orlando. Then Fletch had seen Norival Passarinho really walk after he was dead, really talk. Adroaldo Passarinho. Well it *was* funny.

Fletch was dead. He had died forty-seven years ago. At Dona Jurema's mountain resort the Tap Dancers had tried, maybe as a joke, to arrange a corpse for him. People believed he could answer a question older than himself. Who had murdered Janio Barreto? And he had answered it. Apparently, Fletch had seen mythological figures which were not a part of his own culture. Of course, they must have been just costumed revelers under the stands. Were they? He had helped the dead Norival Passarinho walk, in a crazy, drunken scheme. Then he had believed he saw Norival Passarinho walk, heard him talk. Fletch had come back to life. He was in a closed coffin.

For Fletch, the line between life and death had become narrower. It was so narrow, it really could be funny.

Across the utility area, the man painting the room looked at Fletch.

Fletch had not realized he was staring at the man.

Fletch waved.

Grinning, the man waved back at him. He waved his paintbrush.

Fletch blinked. *He has damned little paint on that paintbrush, if he does not hesitate to wave it at someone, in a room he has been painting for days!*

Fletch laughed.

The man waved his paintbrush again.

Across the utility area the two men laughed together.

Fletch gave the man the thumbs-up sign, then went back into his room.

He telephoned the Hotel Jangada.

Room 912 did not answer.

Mrs. Joan Collins Stanwyk had not checked out.

Yes, there was a message awaiting her in her mail slot.

Drinking mineral water from a plastic liter bottle, Fletch read Laura's note a third time.

Then he called Teodomiro da Costa and arranged to meet with him that night. He would be late, Fletch said, as he intended to drive to the village of Botelho and back.

Teo recommended the seafood restaurant there.

Reluctantly, Fletch knelt. His cuts and bruises protesting, he leaned over until his head was only a few centimeters from the floor.

He peered under the bed.

The small, carved stone frog was gone.

36

"What are you doing here?"

Joan Collins Stanwyk, dressed in shorts which were too big and a T-shirt which had some slogan on it in Portuguese, stood across the rough restaurant table from Fletch.

"Eating."

"But how do you come to be here?"

"I was hungry." He continued eating.

"Really," she said. "How did you find me?"

Her eyes were round in amazement.

"Brazilian police apparently are not always as casual as they like to appear."

The restaurant was a patio with a roof over it on the beach.

"Can you join me?" Fletch asked. "Or aren't the help allowed to sit with the customers."

"I can buy you a cup of coffee," she said.

In sandals, she went across the restaurant to the serving tables.

He had enjoyed the drive through Rio's suburbs, through the Brazilian countryside down the coast. He enjoyed sucking in good air and seeing the real things of the countryside, real rocks and trees, real cows and goats. Good roads had been laid out against the day Brazil's past would catch up with her future. As he drove farther, most of the traffic he passed was on foot.

It had not taken him long to tour the village of Botelho. A short dock poked into a long ocean. The fish warehouse was no more than a shed. In the tiny church was a powerful, crude crucifixion. Less than a dozen fisherfolk bungalows facing the sea dozed in the shade of their own groves.

At the entrance to the open-air seafood restaurant he spotted Joan. Standing with her back to him in the kitchen area, Joan Collins Stanwyk, Mrs. Alan Stanwyk, was placing plates and glasses in a vat of steaming water. He watched her dry her hands and begin shelving clean plates.

It was early for dinner. The only other customers in the restaurant were five fishermen at one table chatting over *chopinhos*. A young waiter gave Fletch a menu and understood as Fletch pointed to a soup and a fish entrée.

Brown paper sack on the bench beside him, Fletch gazed out over the beach to the ocean. Sooner or later, Joan Collins Stanwyk would turn, look through the serving apparatus, see him. He left her the option of ignoring his presence. He would go away again without speaking, if that was what she wanted.

The fish chowder was the best he'd ever had.

He was halfway through his fish entrée when Joan crossed the restaurant and spoke to him.

Now she sat across from him at the long, rough table. She had placed a cup of coffee before each of them.

"I'm glad you're all right," he said, still eating.

"Have an accident?"

"No, thanks. Just had one."

They both laughed nervously.

"You look like someone really beat on you." Especially did her eyes fasten on the small scar on his throat.

"I ran into an enraged nanny goat." Her face put on patience. "That is the story I have decided to tell, to say is the past."

Joan's face looked better than when he saw her Saturday morning. There was good color in her skin and her eyes were clear. So far, she had not lit a cigarette, which was unusual for her. She was wearing no makeup at all. It was also obvious her hair had received little attention in the previous four days.

"It really was good of you to seek me out," Joan said. "Have I been much trouble?"

"I was worried about you. I've been stood up for dinner before, often, but seldom for breakfast."

"Not very nice of me."

"It's okay. I had breakfast anyway."

"Well." She looked into her coffee cup.

"The food here is very good."

"Isn't it? I love it."

"Very good indeed. You wash dishes in this establishment?"

"Yes."

"Didn't think you knew how."

"It's not one of the more artful skills." She showed him her hands. "Aren't they beautiful?" They were red and wrinkled.

"They look honest."

She fluttered her hands and put them in her lap. "I feel like a schoolgirl who's been caught playing hooky."

"It's just nice to know you're alive."

"Any questions I might have had about you and Alan's death ..." She looked into Fletch's face, then at the scar on his neck, then into her own lap. "... I don't have now. The money—"

"I'm willing to do my best to try to explain."

In truth, Fletch wondered if Joan, in her extreme competence, was making some sort of a bargain with him.

"Not necessary," she said. "I know as much as I want to know. I pursued you to Brazil out of some sense of duty." Numbly, she repeated, "Some sense of duty."

He pushed his empty plate away. He realized Joan Collins Stanwyk was expected to wash it.

He sat silently, gazing out to sea. He waited until she understood that he was not questioning her.

She was sitting on her bench, her back straight, leaning on nothing. "I walked away from you that morning, Saturday morning, away from your hotel, to walk to my own hotel. You had said some things I had never heard before. I became angry in a way I had never been angry before.

"Suddenly I realized that here I was, a grown woman, stumbling along in the morning sunlight in tears because someone had stolen my little pins. My pinkie rings! Little plastic cards with my name on them!"

Fletch said, "Also irreplaceable photographs of your husband, Alan, and your daughter, Julie."

"Yes. That profoundly bothers me. But I realized what a spoiled brat I was. I am. Skinny little beggar children were dancing all around me as I walked along, their hands out, whispering at me. I waved my arm at them, and through tight jaws shouted, *Oh, go away!* Couldn't they understand that I had lost a few of my diamonds, my credit cards, to me a negligible amount of cash? How dare they bother me at seven o'clock in the morning for money for food?

"I became truly angry at myself. What a superficial, supercilious bitch. What a hollow person. I had spent the night whining at the poor assistant manager at the hotel. I rushed to you at first light, to whine to you. And here I was virtually swinging at hungry kids."

She said, "Joanie Collins had lost a few pins."

Fletch sipped his coffee.

"Then I had a second thought, based on what you had said." Her index finger was feeling along a short crack in the table. "In a most peculiar way, I was free. I had been relieved of my identity. My credit cards had been stolen, my passport. It almost meant nothing that I was Joan Collins Stanwyk. At least, I couldn't prove it immediately to anybody. I couldn't go up to anybody, in a store or something, and say, 'I'm Joan Collins Stanwyk,' and make it mean anything. As you said, I was just arms and legs: one more person walking naked in the world.

"I liked that thought. Suddenly I liked the idea of being without all that baggage."

From behind the serving apparatus, a tall, slim man was peering out at them. He was looking from Joan to Fletch to Joan again with apparent concern.

Fletch said, "You're still Joan Collins Stanwyk."

"Oh, I know. But, for the first time in my life, it didn't seem to mean much. I saw that it didn't have to mean much."

Again Fletch permitted his question to remain tacit.

"When I got to the Hotel Jangada, a tour bus was waiting. I didn't know where it was going. I joined the people, the women in their short silk dresses, the men in their plaid shorts, and got on it. No one asked me for a ticket, or money. Obviously I belonged to a group from the Hotel Jangada. I belonged with these people. I stole a bus ride here."

Fletch smiled. "Thievery is infectious."

"The bus stopped here for lunch. I didn't have lunch. I couldn't pay for it. What a new fact! What a new feeling! I wandered around the beach. I let the bus leave without me.

"I wondered who I was. Really was. Really am. I wondered if I could survive a full day without cash, without credit cards, without my identity. I wondered what life would be like, for just a few moments, if I couldn't pull something out of my purse and say, 'Here I am, now do as I ask, please; give me ...'" She smiled at herself. "It was getting dark. So I came here and had dinner. I sat over there." She indicated a bench near the door. "I felt as guilty as hell." She put her elbows on the table in a most unrefined way, her chin on her hands. "Then I went and washed dishes for them."

"Is it fun for you?"

"It's harder than tennis. I daydream about having a proper massage. God, last night I wanted a martini so badly." She shrugged. "I can't understand a word of the language. It's so soft, so sibilant."

The tall man, wiping his hands on an apron, finally was approaching them.

Joan's face was happy. She said, "This noon, a well-dressed couple arrived for lunch. German, I think. In a Mercedes, behind a uniformed driver. I found myself looking at her over my pile of dirty dishes. Somehow it made me angry that she only picked at her lunch. Of course I understood. She has to keep her figure ..."

The man stood behind Joan, looking at Fletch. He put his hand on her shoulder.

She put her hand on his.

"Fletch, this is Claudio."

"*Bom dia*, Claudio."

Fletch half rose, and they shook hands.

"Claudio owns this place, I think," Joan said. "At least he acts as if he owns the place. He acts as if he owns the world. It may just be Brazilian masculinity."

Assured she was all right, and apparently without conversation in English, Claudio left the back of his hand against Joan's cheek for a moment, then went back to the kitchen.

"Are you here forever?" Fletch asked. "Have you decided upon dish-washing as a career?"

"Oh, no. Of course not. I love Julie. I love my father. I must get back. I have responsibilities. To Collins Aviation. I'm the best fund raiser Symphony has."

Fletch put the brown paper sack on the table.

"Just leave me here for a while," Joan said quietly. "Let me play truant from life for a short while, from being mother, daughter, from being Joan Collins Stanwyk. Leave me be."

"Sure." He pushed the paper bag across the table at her.

"What's that?" she asked.

"The money I was bringing you Saturday—enhanced by poker earnings. For when you decide to get back." She looked into the bag. "Surely enough to get you back to Rio, pay a hotel bill for a few nights, pay for Telexes."

"How very nice."

"Poverty is easier to slip into," Fletch said, "than to climb out of."

She reached across the table and took his hand. "How do you know so much?"

"Just the wisdom of the masses. Also," he said, "you must still have the key to your suite at the Hotel Jangada."

"I must have. It must be in a pocket of that pants suit I was wearing."

"Get it for me. I'll check you out of the hotel. I'll leave your luggage with the concierge, for when you want it."

"I will want it," she said. "I'm sure I will."

While Fletch paid the waiter, Joan told him about bathing in the warm ocean, how hot the sun was at midday, how much she liked the smell of fish, it was so real, the sounds of something she thought might be tree frogs at night.

"You sound like you're at summer camp," he said.

"No. At summer camp someone else washed the dishes. And," she smiled, "there were only girls."

Fletch waited by his car while she got the key to her suite at the Hotel Jangada. It was still daylight. Customers were beginning to arrive for dinner.

As Joan crossed the small parking lot to him, some of the customers stared after her, perplexed.

"Do me one other favor, will you?" she asked.

"Sure." Fletch had known there would be a second part to the bargain. There are always two parts to a bargain.

"When you go back to the States, to California, back to your own reality, don't ever tell anyone that this crazy thing happened to me, that I did this crazy thing. That you found me washing dishes in a fish joint in some nameless little town in Southern Brazil."

"The town has a name."

She laughed. "You know, I don't know what it is?"

"Botelho."

"Will you promise me that?"

"Sure."

"I mean, everyone needs a vacation from life. Don't you agree?"

"A vacation from reality."

She handed him the key. "I'm paying for a suite at the Hotel Jangada, and sleeping more or less on the beach in Botelho."

Fletch said: "Topsy-turvy."

37

"Did you enjoy your dinner in Botelho?" Teodomiro da Costa asked.

"It was excellent," Fletch answered.

"Yes, that's a good restaurant. I'm not sure it's worth the ride …"

It was late when Fletch got back to Rio, by the time he arrived at Teo da Costa's home on Avenida Epitácio Pessoa.

When the houseman had shown Fletch into the downstairs family sitting room, Teo was looking sleepy in a dressing gown in a comfortable chair. He was reading the book *1887—The Year Slavery in Brazil Ended*. From under the reading light, Teo's eyes traveled over Fletch's various visible wounds, but he did not comment on them.

"Want a nightcap?"

"No, thanks. I won't be here that long."

Stiff from Carnival, from his wounds, from the long ride, Fletch sank comfortably into the two-seater divan.

In the little sitting room was a handsome big new painting by Misabel Pedrosa.

"And did Laura enjoy Botelho?"

"Laura has gone back to Bahia. Yesterday, I finally fell asleep. She couldn't wake me up. She had to go back to begin preparing for her concert tour."

"Yes," Teo said slowly, "I gathered you might have cleaned up that mystery of who murdered Janio Barreto forty-seven years ago. There was a most peculiar report in *O Globo* this morning. A small item, saying Gabriel Campos, past capoeira master of Escola Santos Lima, was found on the beach, his throat slit. A woman from the favela, Idalina Barreto, is helping the police in its inquiries."

"I pity the police."

"Apparently she was found on the beach lighting matches, trying to set fire to the corpse of Gabriel Campos."

"Did she succeed?"

"That's what's peculiar about *O Globo*'s report. It says that legend has it that no one has ever succeeded in lighting a fire in that exact spot on the beach in almost fifty years."

"Teo, I'd like some of the money you've invested for me to be available for the education of the current young generation of the descendants of Janio Barreto."

"Easily done."

"Especially young Janio. He has a wooden leg. It will be harder for him to make a living without an education."

"Yes."

Fletch fingered the scar on his throat. "I believe he saved my life." Then he chuckled. "He might even think of becoming a bookkeeper."

Teo placed his history book on the table beside his chair. "And did you find your lady friend from California? What's her name, Stanwyk?"

"Yes. She's all right."

"What happened to her?"

"She fell out of her cradle. She's enjoying a few moments crawling around the floor."

Obviously tired, Teo cast his hooded eye across the darkened room at Fletch.

"Brazil is the future," Fletch said. "Who can see the future?"

"And you," Teo asked, shifting comfortably in his chair. "Did you enjoy Carnival?"

"I learned some things."

"I'd love to know what."

"Oh, that the past asserts itself. That the dead can walk." Fletch thought of the small carved stone frog that had been under his bed. "That the absence of symbols can mean as much as their presence."

As if digesting all this, Teo blinked his hooded eye. He did not ask questions.

"Teo, driving so far today by myself, through the incredible Brazilian countryside, I think I settled on a plan."

"No need to tell me what it is," Teo said. "Anymore than there is to tell your father what it is. As long as you have a plan."

"I've decided to try writing a biography of the North American western artist Edgar Arthur Tharp Junior. It seems an opportunity to get some things said about the North American's view of the artist, the intellectual, of the North American spirit."

Teo repeated, "As long as you have a plan."

"It is the spirit of things which is important, isn't it?"

Teo said, "Norival Passarinho's funeral is tomorrow. Will you attend?"

Fletch hesitated. "Yes." He stood up. "Why not?"

Teo stood up as well. "And will you visit Bahia before you leave?"

At the door, Fletch said: "To say good-bye."

FOR A MOMENT, Fletch sat quietly in the dark in the small yellow convertible outside Teodomiro da Costa's home.

A few doors from Teo's, a last Carnival party was in progress. It was Shrove Tuesday night.

A couple dressed as the King of Hearts and the Queen of Diamonds scurried across the sidewalk from a taxi into the house.

There was the sound of laughter coming from the house. Singing. Above all, the sound of a samba combo. *Of samba drums beating, rhythms beside rhythms on top of rhythms beneath rhythms. From all sides, every minute, day and night, came the beating of the drums.*

"*Bum, bum, paticum bum.*" Fletch started the car. "*Prugurundum.*"

Most people in the world Fletch had known had stopped hearing the melodies from the drums.

GREGORY MCDONALD (1937–2008) insisted that he was educated while earning his way through Harvard by creating and running an international yacht trouble-shooting business. A former *Boston Globe* reporter, he won two Edgar Allan Poe Awards for his writing as well as numerous awards for humanitarian work.